BREAKAWAY BLISS

(An Ashville Aces Hockey Romance —Book One)

FIONA GRACE

Fiona Grace

Fiona Grace is author of the LACEY DOYLE COZY MYSTERY series, comprising nine books; of the TUSCAN VINEYARD COZY MYSTERY series, comprising seven books; of the DUBIOUS WITCH COZY MYSTERY series, comprising three books; of the BEACHFRONT BAKERY COZY MYSTERY series, comprising six books; of the CATS AND DOGS COZY MYSTERY series, comprising nine books; of the ELIZA MONTAGU COZY MYSTERY series, comprising nine books (and counting); of the ENDLESS HARBOR ROMANTIC COMEDY series, comprising nine books (and counting); of the INN AT DUNE ISLAND ROMANTIC COMEDY series, comprising seven books (and counting); of the INN BY THE SEA ROMANTIC COMEDY series, comprising five books (and counting); of the MAID AND THE MANSION COZY MYSTERY series, comprising five books (and counting); of the ALICE BLOOM COZY MYSTERY series, comprising five books (and counting); of the MAGNOLIA BAY COZY MYSTERY series, comprising five books (and counting); of the TIMBERLAKE TITANS HOCKEY ROMANCE series, comprising five books (and counting); and of the ASHVILLE ACES HOCKEY ROMANCE series, comprising five books (and counting).

Fiona would love to hear from you, so please visit www.fionagraceauthor.com to receive free ebooks, hear the latest news, and stay in touch.

ISBN: 979-8-89482-528-1

BOOKS BY FIONA GRACE

ASHVILLE ACES HOCKEY ROMANCE
BREAKAWAY BLISS (Book #1)
ICY INTIMACY (Book #2)
FACEOFF FLING (Book #3)
RINK RENDEZVOUS (Book #4)
HOCKEY HEARTTHROB (Book #5)

TIMBERLAKE TITANS HOCKEY ROMANCE
RINKSIDE ROMANCE (Book #1)
FLIRTY FACEOFF (Book #2)
MELTING THE ICE (Book #3)
THE PUCK STOPS HERE (Book #4)
GLOVES DROP, LOVE BLOOMS (Book #5)

MAGNOLIA BAY COZY MYSTERY
THE TAINTED TAFFY (Book #1)
A MASKED MURDER (Book #2)
A CAFE CONFESSION (Book #3)
THE FROZEN FIND (Book #4)
A CURIOUS CURSE (Book #5)

THE MAID AND THE MANSION COZY MYSTERY
A MYSTERIOUS MURDER (Book #1)
A SCANDALOUS DEATH (Book #2)
A MISSING GUEST (Book #3)
AN UNSOLVABLE CRIME (Book #4)
AN IMPOSSIBLE HEIST (Book #5)

INN BY THE SEA ROMANTIC COMEDY
A NEW LOVE (Book #1)
A NEW CHANCE (Book #2)
A NEW HOME (Book #3)
A NEW LIFE (Book #4)
A NEW ME (Book #5)

THE INN AT DUNE ISLAND ROMANTIC COMEDY
A CHANCE LOVE (Book #1)
A CHANCE FALL (Book #2)
A CHANCE ROMANCE (Book #3)
A CHANCE CHRISTMAS (Book #4)
A CHANCE ENGAGEMENT (Book #5)
A CHANCE DREAM (Book #6)
A CHANCE WEDDING (Book #7)

ENDLESS HARBOR ROMANTIC COMEDY
ALWAYS, WITH YOU (Book #1)
ALWAYS, FOREVER (Book #2)
ALWAYS, PLUS ONE (Book #3)
ALWAYS, TOGETHER (Book #4)
ALWAYS, LIKE THIS (Book #5)
ALWAYS, FATED (Book #6)
ALWAYS, FOR LOVE (Book #7)
ALWAYS, JUST US (Book #8)
ALWAYS, IN LOVE (Book #9)

ELIZA MONTAGU COZY MYSTERY
MURDER AT THE HEDGEROW (Book #1)
A DALLOP OF DEATH (Book #2)
CALAMITY AT THE BALL (Book #3)
A SPEAKEASY DEMISE (Book #4)
A FLAPPER FATALITY (Book #5)
BUMPED BY A DAME (Book #6)
A DOLL'S DEBACLE (Book #7)
A FELLA'S RUIN (Book #8)
A GAL'S OFFING (Book #9)

LACEY DOYLE COZY MYSTERY
MURDER IN THE MANOR (Book#1)
DEATH AND A DOG (Book #2)
CRIME IN THE CAFE (Book #3)
VEXED ON A VISIT (Book #4)
KILLED WITH A KISS (Book #5)
PERISHED BY A PAINTING (Book #6)
SILENCED BY A SPELL (Book #7)
FRAMED BY A FORGERY (Book #8)
CATASTROPHE IN A CLOISTER (Book #9)

TUSCAN VINEYARD COZY MYSTERY
AGED FOR MURDER (Book #1)
AGED FOR DEATH (Book #2)
AGED FOR MAYHEM (Book #3)
AGED FOR SEDUCTION (Book #4)
AGED FOR VENGEANCE (Book #5)
AGED FOR ACRIMONY (Book #6)
AGED FOR MALICE (Book #7)

DUBIOUS WITCH COZY MYSTERY
SKEPTIC IN SALEM: AN EPISODE OF MURDER (Book #1)
SKEPTIC IN SALEM: AN EPISODE OF CRIME (Book #2)
SKEPTIC IN SALEM: AN EPISODE OF DEATH (Book #3)

BEACHFRONT BAKERY COZY MYSTERY
BEACHFRONT BAKERY: A KILLER CUPCAKE (Book #1)
BEACHFRONT BAKERY: A MURDEROUS MACARON (Book #2)
BEACHFRONT BAKERY: A PERILOUS CAKE POP (Book #3)
BEACHFRONT BAKERY: A DEADLY DANISH (Book #4)
BEACHFRONT BAKERY: A TREACHEROUS TART (Book #5)
BEACHFRONT BAKERY: A CALAMITOUS COOKIE (Book #6)

CATS AND DOGS COZY MYSTERY
A VILLA IN SICILY: OLIVE OIL AND MURDER (Book #1)
A VILLA IN SICILY: FIGS AND A CADAVER (Book #2)
A VILLA IN SICILY: VINO AND DEATH (Book #3)
A VILLA IN SICILY: CAPERS AND CALAMITY (Book #4)
A VILLA IN SICILY: ORANGE GROVES AND VENGEANCE (Book #5)
A VILLA IN SICILY: CANNOLI AND A CASUALTY (Book #6)

ALICE BLOOM COZY MYSTERY
MURDER IN THE MARIGOLDS (Book #1)
RUIN IN THE ROSES (Book #2)
DECEIT IN THE DAFFODILS (Book #3)
SCANDAL IN THE SAFFRON (Book #4)
CATASTROPHE IN THE CARNATIONS (Book #5)

CHAPTER ONE: LEXI

My heart does a triple axel in my chest as I step into the frigid embrace of Ashville College's hockey arena. First day jitters skate circles around my stomach, but excitement pumps through my veins like adrenaline before a big game. It's a cocktail of emotions, but I'm ready to drink it down. Sure, Ashville, Minnesota isn't exactly everyone; idea of a great place to start a sports career, but my hometown holds its own.

Senior year. This internship is one of the only things between me and fulfilling my degree requirements. I'm *so* ready.

"Okay, Lexi," I mutter to myself, "time to make 'em proud."

With every stride across the gleaming concourse, I can feel the ghosts of hockey legends past whispering in my ear, reminding me this is where I belong. I breathe in the familiar scent of cold air mixed with the faint musk of Zamboni exhaust—smells like *potential.*

I don't waste time. The layout of the arena unfolds before me like one of those schematic diagrams my dad used to draw up for game plays. To the left, the locker rooms with their promise of sweaty gear and strategy talks; straight ahead, the training rooms humming with the reminders of rehabbed injuries; and beyond that, the rink itself—a shimmering expanse of ice that's seen more slice than a pizzeria on game night.

"Home sweet home," I say under my breath, a smirk playing at the corner of my mouth.

I imagine Dad's voice coaching me through this moment, the same way he did when I laced up my first pair of skates. "Keep your head up, Lexi. Eyes on the play." It's a mantra for hockey and, as it turns out, life.

The arena is quiet now, though the whole Ashville Aces team is either on the ice or leaning on the outside of the boards—the calm before the storm of stick-clashing and puck-slapping practice. I take a mental snapshot of each player, though they are small from where I'm at in the stands, and each area, storing them in my mind next to all the sports medicine knowledge I've been hoarding for years. This isn't just some internship. It's the first shift of the rest of my career, and I want to be ready for anything.

"Show them what you're made of, Turner," I pep-talk myself, brushing a loose strand of hair back into my ponytail as I start down the steps toward the rink.

like the memory of a thousand early morning practices. The sharp sound of blades cutting across the surface echoes through the arena, a symphony to any hockey lover's ears. I'm close enough to see the players' breaths hang in the air, their determined faces set and focused.

"Alexis Turner?" A voice booms over the ambient noise. I turn to find the source—a man with a presence that fills the space around him. Coach Thompson stands there, barrel-chested, military-cut gray hair, khakis and long-sleeves polo impeccable, clipboard in hand, wearing a look that means business.

"Call me Lexi," I respond, extending my hand. My grip is firm, practiced; it has to be when you're stepping into a world dominated by men who could bench press your body weight.

"Right, Lexi." He clasps my hand with a nod, appraising me for a moment too long, slightly wary. "Welcome aboard. Our physio, Drew, will typically be joining us when you're here. But today, it's just us. Let's introduce you to the team."

We weave between the benches and discarded water bottles until we're at the edge of the rink. The practice is now in full swing—players weaving intricate patterns on the ice, puck flying from stick to stick with a precision that speaks of endless drills.

"Everyone!" Coach Thompson's voice cuts through the clatter. Practice slows as players circle around us, curiosity lighting up their sweat-glistened faces. "This is Lexi, our new intern. She'll be assisting with physical therapies and ensuring you lot don't fall apart mid-season."

I look over the team, noting each man as I recognize him. I've studied the roster and the team's online portfolios.

Tyler Reed, defenseman.

Chris Anderson, center.

Dean "The Machine" Hartley, Kyle "Flash" Franklin, Alexander "Xander" Price, "Reckless" Reid Jackson—wingers *always* have nicknames.

And Eric Larson, goalie.

A chorus of nods and murmurs greet me. None of them are too enthusiastic. And then, Noah Bishop, the captain, skates forward with an ease that speaks volumes of his time on the ice. His smile is genuine, welcoming; it makes something in my chest loosen.

"Nice to meet you, Lexi," he says, his voice calm and reassuring.

"Likewise," I reply, but before I can say more, another figure commands attention.

Wes Jacobs, star forward, swishes closer with a swagger that takes up more space than it should. There's a challenge in his ice-blue eyes, visible even through his helmet, the kind that says he knows exactly how good he is. But underneath the bravado, I see something else—a flicker of something deeper.

"Hope you've got thick skin," Wes says, his tone teasing but edged with a dare. "Some of us aren't as easygoing as Captain America here."

"Thick skin, steel-toed boots, and a no-nonsense attitude," I shoot back, standing my ground. "I think I'll manage."

A grin tugs at the corner of his mouth, and for a second, I wonder if Wes Jacobs is impressed. But then the moment's gone, lost to the echo of the coach's whistle signaling the end of the huddle.

"Let's get back to it, gentlemen," Coach Thompson announces, and just like that, the players disperse, returning to the rhythm of practice.

I retreat to the sidelines, pulling out my notepad. It's time to observe, to study the way they move individually and together. Noah leads with a calm assertiveness, his play clean and precise. In contrast, Wes is all fire and flash, pushing the limits with a natural instinct that can't be taught. But he also takes risks—risks that can get him hurt, in the wrong circumstance. The dynamic on the ice is readable, the push and pull of personalities and play styles. They're a unit, yes, but within it are stories, rivalries, friendships. I scribble down notes on their techniques, already thinking of training programs, injury prevention strategies.

They think they're just showing off for the new girl, but I'm seeing much more than that. I'm seeing potential. They all move well together, and I'm seeing the beginning of an unforgettable season—if they can keep it together.

The last few minutes of practice is when it happens.

They're running drills again, a two-on-two scrimmage, Bishop and Jacobs against Anderson and Reed. The puck dances between sticks, gliding across the ice with a mesmerizing rhythm. Noah has control, the puck seemingly attracted to his stick as he weaves through the makeshift defense. He's about to pass it over to Wes when it happens.

Wes charges forward without looking, shoulder colliding hard into Noah's chest. It's a brutal impact, a thunderous clash of bodies that sends shockwaves through the rink. Both players hit the ice in an unceremonious tumble, leaving silence in its wake.

I gasp along with everyone else.

Wes is the first to move, pushing himself up. He looks over at Noah, his eyes wide with shock. The puck rests forgotten a few feet away. Around us, the entire rink holds its breath.

"Bishop, you all right?" Wes is kneeling next to him now, his usual bravado replaced by concern.

Noah groans and tries to push himself up with a grunt. "Yeah," he finally says, his voice edged with annoyance. "Dude, you hit me like a ton of bricks."

The collective breath of everyone in the arena seems to whoosh out as Wes helps Noah to his feet, and they rerun the drill without incident. But I see it—Noah's favoring one of his ankles. A shrill whistle pierces the arena, signaling a break in practice. Players glide to the boards, chests heaving, sweat glistening on their brows. I push off the wall, my sneakers finding traction as I make my way across the rubber mats toward Noah, who's wincing, sat in the penalty box, one hand clutched around his ankle.

"Hey, Noah," I say, pitching my voice above the din of exhausted chatter. "Mind if I take a look at that?"

Maybe I shouldn't—the team physio isn't here to oversee me. I wonder if I'm being too bold. I don't want to get into trouble day one, but I'm here, and I can help.

Noah looks up, surprise etching his features—which are, admittedly, pretty cute now that I have a clear view of him without the face guard in the way—before he masks it with a grin that doesn't quite reach his eyes. "Offering your expertise on the first day? Do I get this VIP treatment often?"

"Only when you're limping like a pirate with a peg leg," I retort, kneeling beside him. His skate is already off, and my fingers are deft as they peel back his sock, exposing an ankle that's already swelling. "How bad is it?"

"Ah, I've had worse." His attempt at nonchalance doesn't fool me. The grimace gives him away as I probe gently.

"Scale of one to ten?" I ask, keeping my touch light but clinical as I assess the damage.

"Solid six?" He winces again as I press a tender spot.

"Previous injuries?" My mind races through potential treatments even as I await his response.

"A sprain last season. Same ankle." Noah's gaze holds mine, a silent understanding passing between us. He knows I'm not just another intern; I know what this game costs.

"All right, Captain," I say, injecting confidence into my tone. "Let's get some ice on this and talk to Coach."

I return quickly with a bag of ice and an Ace bandage, my mind whirring with treatment plans. Noah watches me approach, his expression a blend of gratitude and pain that tugs at something deep inside me. I've always been a sucker for the wounded-hero type, but it's more than that—his worry is practically etched into his features.

"All right, Captain," I begin, easing down beside him. "Let's turn that six into a two, shall we?" My hands are steady as I wrap the ice in a towel before positioning it against his ankle.

"Is this the part where you tell me my season's over and I should start considering underwater basket weaving as a sport?" Noah jokes, that charming half-smile playing on his lips.

"Only if you're planning to make it a contact sport. Otherwise, I don't think hockey fans will follow you to your next endeavor." I secure the bandage with practiced ease. "But seriously, keep weight off it for the next 24 hours, ice for twenty minutes on, forty off. And I'll need you doing some light rehab exercises starting tomorrow."

"Bossy, aren't you?" he teases, but he nods, showing he's taking it all in.

"Comes with the territory. And Coach Thompson did say I'm here to help, remember? But I guess you're used to calling the shots, huh? How does it feel to be on the other side?"

"Surprisingly refreshing," he admits, watching me work with keen blue eyes. "You have a good touch, Lexi. Not too gentle, not too rough. Goldilocks would approve."

"Let's not bring fairy tales into this," I quip, adjusting the ice pack. "Although, if you want, I can recite 'Jack and the Beanstalk' while you elevate your leg. I know it by heart. I did a lot of babysitting for extra cash my freshman year."

"Thanks, I'll pass." He laughs, the sound rich and warm, and for a brief moment, we're just two people sharing a joke instead of an intern and team captain in the middle of a hockey arena. It's strangely intimate, this shared bubble of levity.

"All right then, no bedtime stories." I stand up, brushing off my hands as I offer him a final piece of advice. "Remember, RICE—rest, ice, compression, elevation. Stick to it, and you'll be terrorizing opponents on the ice again before you know it."

"Wes is the terror—and you notice he's fled the scene of the crime?"

I nod, looking around for the other crash-ee. We must be in the locker room already. Noah's ankle, now neatly wrapped and iced, looks like a textbook example of sprain management. I step back, hands on hips, surveying my handiwork.

"I see that. Well, that should do it," I say, checking off mental notes in my head. "How's the pressure? Not too tight, I hope."

Noah flexes his ankle gingerly, testing the limits of the compression tape holding the ice in place. "It's perfect," he admits with a nod of approval. "You really know your stuff, Lexi."

"Thanks," I reply, trying to brush off the compliment with nonchalance, even though inside I'm doing victory laps. "Just doing my job."

"Still," Noah continues, sincerity lacing his voice, "I've had my fair share of ankle sprains, and this feels better than most wraps I've had. You're not just going through the motions—you actually care. It makes a difference."

His words, warm and appreciative, ignite a little spark of pride in my chest. The captain of the hockey team acknowledging my dedication is more than just a confidence booster—it's validation that I'm exactly where I'm meant to be.

"Appreciate it, Captain," I quip with a wink. "Now, don't go ruining my masterpiece by playing hero on the ice before you're ready."

"Wouldn't dream of it," he chuckles, but there's a promise in his eyes that tells me he'll heed my advice.

"You going to live, Cap?" A deep voice cuts through our exchange, and I turn to find Wes Jacobs leaning against the doorframe of the penalty box. His presence is like a sudden drop in temperature, the air charged with a different kind of electricity.

"He'll be fine," I respond, crossing my arms over my chest. I'm all too aware of his reputation—Wes Jacobs doesn't play by anyone's rules but his own. He certainly didn't stick around to see if Noah was okay, and I don't recall him apologizing for causing the collision.

"Nice job with the ankle," Wes says, eyeing Noah's foot with a hint of skepticism. "But come on, isn't all this a bit much? Do we even need someone like you hovering over us? Walk it off—that's how real players handle it."

"Is that so?" I challenge, meeting his intense gaze head-on. He might unnerve others, but I grew up with three brothers who taught me how to stand my ground. "Because 'real players' also have 'real career-ending injuries' when they ignore professional medical advice."

I maintain eye contact with Wes, noting the stubborn set of his jaw as I calmly lay out the facts. "Every player thinks they're invincible until they're not," I continue, my voice steady despite his challenging stare. "Ignoring a minor injury can lead to major setbacks. Trust me, you don't want to be benched because you played tough instead of smart."

He surveys me with cool amusement. "So, what's your grand plan to keep us from breaking apart? Bubble wrap under our jerseys?"

"Only for the biggest egos," I retort quickly. “Let me know what size jersey you wear so I can order plenty.” My response seems to crack the ice, and Wes's lips twitch into a reluctant grin.

"Okay, Doc," he concedes, the nickname laced with a hint of respect. "I'll bite. What do you suggest?"

"Preventative care," I say, seizing the opportunity. "Proper warm-ups, cool-downs, regular check-ups, and listening to your body. It's not rocket science, but it works."

Wes nods slowly, and I can tell he's actually considering my words. "And if we still end up injured?" he challenges.

"Then you'll have the best care I can give. But let's try to avoid that, shall we?" I offer him a smile that's part professional, part playful, hoping to bridge the gap between his defiance and my dedication.

Wes pushes off from the doorway, stepping closer with a smirk that could either mean trouble or interest—I can't tell which. "Well, then, I guess we'll see how good you really are at keeping this bunch of misfits in one piece."

"Challenge accepted," I shoot back, refusing to let his jibe rattle me. There's something about Wes Jacobs that spells complication, but I'm not one to back down from a fight—especially not on my first day.

"Fair enough," he admits, pushing off the wall and heading toward the rink. "We'll see what you've got, Turner."

Watching him skate away, I turn my attention back to Noah, who's been quietly observing our exchange. His approving nod fills me with a sense of accomplishment; I've managed to handle Wes Jacobs, at least for now.

"Seems like you might just survive this internship," Noah comments, the warmth in his voice contrasting sharply with Wes's earlier chill.

"Survive?" I laugh. "I'm planning to thrive."

"Good luck," Noah says with a knowing look. "You're gonna need it with him."

"Thanks," I reply, "but I have a feeling luck has nothing to do with it."

There's much to learn about this team, about these players, and how they mesh together on and off the ice. But one thing's for certain—it's going to be one heck of a season.

CHAPTER TWO: NOAH

A sprained ankle is the least of my worries right now—though thoughts of the woman who'd just tended to me is edging out some of those anxieties.

The weight of the 'C' on my chest is a constant reminder of what's at stake. With each game, there's a pressure that mounts, tightening around me like the laces of my skates. It's not just about winning; it's about leading these guys to victory, making sure we're more than a team—more like a brotherhood, where every pass and check on the ice is built on trust.

I'm in the training room early, the quiet before the storm of grunts and clattering equipment. The faint smell of antiseptic fights against the lingering scent of sweat—a testament to yesterday's practice. On the walls, there are posters with motivational quotes that I can practically recite in my sleep. But today, none of them seem to penetrate the haze of my concentration as I think about tonight's game. We need this win. I need this win.

My thoughts scatter when the door swings open with a purposeful push. Lexi strides in, her sandy blonde hair pulled back into a practical ponytail that somehow manages to look effortlessly stylish. She scans the room, taking in the scene with a level of focus that rivals any athlete's, before landing on me. There's this thing she does—this narrowing of her eyes—that makes it feel like she's seeing right through to the playbook in my mind. I caught it yesterday, but now, its reappearance makes it clear that it's habitual. And pretty cute.

Unfortunately, she's followed by Drew Carson, the team physio. The logical part of me knows he's supposed to be her supervision during the internship, but there's a part of me that is disgruntled that the tall, lanky staff member is going to be hovering over my alone time with a pretty girl.

"Hey, Drew," I say.

"Noah," he says, nodding at me. He's smirking like he knows exactly why I'm annoyed at his presence.

"Morning, Captain," she says, and there's that edge of sarcasm that tells me she's ready to get down to business and not play around.

"Lexi," I greet, pushing up from the bench and feeling a sense of anticipation bubbling within me. I watch her set down her bag and pull out her supplies, each movement precise and confident. She's like a coach in her own right, calling the shots in the realm of strains and sprains, a general on the battlefield of bodily wear and tear.

"Ready for the big game?" she asks, glancing over her shoulder with a quirked eyebrow that suggests she already knows the answer.

"Always," I reply, but it comes out more like a question, betraying the storm of doubts swirling inside me.

She gives me a knowing nod, as if she's just read the play-by-play of my thoughts, and I can't help but wonder how someone who's never laced up for a college game with the stakes we face seems to understand it all so well. Then again, growing up with a hockey coach for a dad and a high school career on the ice probably taught her more about the game than most.

I admit—I internet snooped a little.

"Good," she says, pulling on her gloves with a snap that echoes off the walls. "Because we've got work to do. Her tone is professional yet not devoid of warmth. "Show me your ankle."

I extend my foot toward her, trying to ignore the way my heart rate kicks up a notch as she kneels. It's ridiculous, really, how someone whose job is literally to inflict pain—or at least discomfort—can make me so damn nervous. Drew's just leaning on the wall behind her, observing.

"Looks like you're favoring your left side." Her fingers are deft, probing the bruised ankle with a gentleness that belies her firm touch. "You know, for a big, tough hockey player, you're surprisingly fragile."

"Hey now," I protest, but there's laughter in my voice. "One more crack like that and I might start thinking you don't believe in my invincibility."

"Invincibility is overrated," Lexi retorts, securing compression tape around my leg with practiced ease. "It's all about resilience, Noah."

"Is that your professional opinion?" I ask, raising an eyebrow.

"Absolutely." She meets my gaze squarely, the ghost of a smile playing on her lips.

I swing my leg up, testing the range of motion in my ankle. It's better already—Lexi's magic hands at work. I can't help the grin that spreads across my face.

"Thanks, Doc," I say, offering her a mock salute. "I wouldn't want to risk further injury by disappointing you."

"Make sure you don't," she replies, pointing a stern finger at me. "I've got enough on my plate without having to patch up our star captain because he couldn't follow simple instructions."

"Simple is my middle name," I assure her, though we both know it's a bald-faced lie. There's nothing simple about the way I play—on the ice or off.

"Good to know," Lexi says, tossing her hair back into a ponytail. "Just remember, Noah Bishop: simplicity doesn't mean taking shortcuts, especially not when it comes to recovery."

"Understood, Coach Turner," I respond with a playful smirk.

"Coach? Ha! Smart man," she says, her eyes twinkling. She looks over her shoulder at Drew, who gives her a thumbs-up.

"You did perfect, Lexi. Noah, any questions for me?"

I shake my head. I don't want to ask him if he could butt out of the next session between me and Lexi.

"Okay, then. See you out there." With a final nod, she strides out of the training room, leaving me to ponder just how much trouble I'm in for being so thoroughly intrigued by our team intern. But for the next couple hours, we're both here for one thing: to make sure me all of The Aces are at our best when we hit the ice. Anything else—like the way my pulse quickens whenever she's around—has to be left on the sidelines.

***

The staccato rhythm of my skates against the ice merges with the thud of pucks hitting the boards, creating a symphony that's both exhilarating and grueling. Each sharp turn sends a jolt through my bruised ankle, but it's the kind of pain that fuels me, reminds me I'm alive and fighting for every point, every game.

"Keep your head up, Bishop!" Coach yells from across the rink, and I nod, knowing full well the target on my back isn't just metaphorical. The title of captain comes with its own set of bullseyes—each check against the boards a testament to that fact. Weakness won't allow me to hold onto the position.

"Nice shot, Noah!" Dean hollers, his voice tinged with sarcasm as my puck narrowly misses the net. I shoot him a glare, but there's no real heat in it. We're teammates, after all, even if he does earn his nickname "The Machine" for reasons that extend beyond the rink.

My confidence in my own infallibility lasts most of practice. By the end of it, I'm in pain again. Practice winds down, and with each stride to the bench, I feel the weight of the game more acutely—the physical toll unmistakable. My muscles protest, reluctant to give in to the exhaustion, while my ankle throbs in time with my heartbeat.

The chill of the training room contrasts starkly with the heat from my muscles, still humming from the morning drills. I perch on the edge of the treatment table, rolling my sprained ankle in slow circles as Lexi approaches. I wonder why she chose this—patching up players in what must get to be a strange déjà vu of injuries.

Drew isn't anywhere to be seen.

"Lose your chaperone?" I tease.

"He's talking to Coach. I guess he trusts me not to hurt you."

I laugh. "That's a vote of confidence, I guess."

"Looks like you took quite a beating today," Lexi observes as I slump before her.

"Just another day at the office," I quip, wincing as she prods gently along my lower leg.

"Ah, the glamorous life of a hockey player," she responds, her hands working deftly, the coolness of the therapeutic gel seeping into my skin. There's a methodical precision in her touch, a silent promise to mend what's been broken—or at least battered—in the rink.

"Can't complain," I say, though my grimace likely tells a different story.

"Sure, because getting slammed into the boards is everyone's idea of a good time," she counters, a smirk playing on her lips. For a moment, I'm caught off guard by the overhead lights catching in her sandy blonde hair, casting a halo around her focused expression.

"You know, you don't always have to be the indestructible Captain America," she says softly, her hands steady as she examines the swelling under her fingers.

"Feels like I do." The words slip out, echoing the doubt that's been gnawing at me. "There's a lot riding on these shoulders."

"Pressure of being captain?" She looks up at me, and there's an understanding in her gaze that makes something inside me want to reveal parts of myself I usually keep locked away.

"Every game feels like a proving ground," I admit, allowing vulnerability to seep into our bubble of trainer and athlete. "I can't slip up. Can't show weakness. Not just for me, but for the team, the fans..."

"Sounds exhausting," she murmurs, her touch gentle as she applies a cold compress to my wrist.

"Only when I think about it." I give her a half-hearted smile.

"Then stop thinking," Lexi advises with a chuckle, but her hand lingers on my leg for a moment longer than necessary.

Our eyes lock, and there's a silent conversation happening—one that's about more than sprains and strategy. In the span of that gaze, the world slows down, and I'm acutely aware of the warmth of her hand, the depth of her eyes, and the faint scent of her shampoo that seems to say, 'pay attention, this is important.'

"Better now?" she asks, breaking the spell but leaving an aftershock of tension between us.

"Much," I say, though I'm not referring to the ankle anymore. There's an electricity in the air, crackling with the potential of what-ifs and maybes. "Have you considered that bubble wrap uniform upgrade?" I tease, hoping to keep my tone light despite the growing tightness in my chest that has nothing to do with injuries.

"Wouldn't want to hinder your performance," Lexi retorts, meeting my gaze with those piercing green eyes. "You need to be able to move, right? Besides, that was your pal Wes's suggestion, and isn't he the one who got you into this position in the first place?" She looks pointedly at my ankle.

"Kind of," I agree, trying to ignore the way even our casual banter seems to charge the air between us. It's a dangerous game we're playing, one where the line between professional and personal blurs. I definitely don't miss the vitriol she has for Wes. They've started off on the wrong foot, for sure.

"Thanks." I watch as she stands. "You ever miss being out there? On the ice, I mean."

"Every day," she confesses with a wistful smile. "But this—helping you guys stay on your feet—that's my new arena."

"That's a noble trade," I say, meeting her gaze. There's something about being here, in the thick of hockey, that makes talking to Lexi feel like the most natural thing in the world. "So, what's the dream, Lexi? After graduation?"

"Pro teams, hopefully," she replies. "I want to be on the front lines, making sure injuries don't end careers prematurely."

"Like yours..." I trail off, remembering her story. I hope she doesn't ask how I know about her knee injury, all those years ago.

Her eyes shadow, but she smiles. "Exactly. I can't play anymore, but I can give others the chance to keep playing. Maybe even prevent what happened to me from happening to someone else."

"That's... really admirable," I tell her, impressed by her determination and passion. I never realized how much our aspirations paralleled—me, striving to lead my team to victory; her, working to safeguard the players' futures.

"Enough about me," Lexi says, nudging my shoulder lightly. "What about you, Noah? What's your endgame?"

"Professional leagues, if I'm lucky. But honestly," I pause, choosing my words, "I just want to inspire people. To show that leadership isn't about bossing others around—it's about lifting them up, being someone they can rely on."

"Sounds like you're already there, Captain," she teases, but I can see the respect in her eyes.

"Trying to be," I admit, and in that admission, I feel a bond forming between us.

"Rest tonight, and ice every two hours," she instructs, snapping me back to reality. “And good practice.”

"Couldn't have done it without your magic hands," I retort, trying to keep it light, keep it safe. But the moment stretches between us, filled with unspoken words and stifled desires.

"See you tomorrow, Captain," she says, her tone casual, but there's something new in her gaze—a flicker of curiosity. “At game time.”

"Tomorrow," I echo, watching her walk away, every step she takes simultaneously pulling me closer and reminding me of the line we're both toeing.

As the training room comes alive with my teammates' raucous energy, I sit there, trapped in the silent tumult of my racing heart and the unanswered question that hangs heavily in the air. Lexi Turner—what happens next?

CHAPTER THREE: WES

The puck's a live wire under my stick, the crowd's roar a tidal wave behind me. I'm in the zone—dekes smooth as silk, skates slicing the ice like it's butter. There's something about the rink that makes everything else fade away; it's just me, the ice, and the game. The scoreboard is tight, but my muscles are loose, coiled springs ready to unleash.

"Jacobs, heads up!" That's Thompson from the bench, his warning barely cuts through the din of the arena. I glance up, just in time to see the opposing team's defense barrel toward me, grim determination etched on his face. Guy's got more beef than a butcher shop, and he's aiming every pound directly at me.

I try for a sidestep—a move I've pulled off a thousand times before—but the guy's like a force of nature, unpredictable and wild. Our collision is thunderous, a meeting of titans, and I feel the jolt right through my shoulder. It's like a dark whisper from my past, a reminder of battles fought and the fragility beneath this armor of muscle and sinew.

"Damn," I hiss, the pain sharp but familiar. Mom's voice echoes in the back of my mind, a relentless mix of worry and pride. "Don't you go hurting yourself now, Wes." But pain's an old friend, one that knows when to show up uninvited. One I know how to push aside—have learned to.

My breath comes out in a foggy burst as I push off the ice, refusing to let the opposition see any flicker of weakness. My shoulder screams a protest, but I've played through worse. Gritting my teeth, I lock eyes with that defender as I circle away, my stride still strong, my resolve even stronger. I've taken hits from life harder than anything this player can dish out, and I'm not about to start backing down now.

"Nice try, princess," I spit out, the words sharp as skate blades. "Gonna take more than that to bench me."

The puck's back in play, and so am I. It's a dance, a battle, a test of wills, and I'm not conceding this game—not to the other team, not to my shoulder, not to anyone. Hockey's in my blood, my escape from the world and all its heavy expectations. This ice is mine, and I'll defend it with everything I've got.

"Keep your head up, Jacobs," I remind myself, stealing a glance at the clock. Time's slipping by, each second another chance to prove I'm unstoppable. Because when it comes down to it, this isn't just about the game. It's about proving to that kid from Minneapolis that he's made of tougher stuff—that he can rise above every hit, every fall, every setback.

For mom, for me, for the sheer thrill of it—I'm not just playing hockey. I'm living it. And nothing, not even a shoulder that feels like it's been through a meat grinder, can change that.

The sharp sting is sudden, a rebellion in my muscles that lights up my nerves like a Christmas tree on fire. Gritting my teeth, I pivot on the ice, feeling the familiar burn that's become an unwanted companion over the years. It's a searing sensation, clawing its way from the deep recesses of my shoulder joint, spreading with every movement I dare to make.

"Shake it off," I mutter under my breath, flexing my fingers and rolling my shoulder in a futile attempt to dismiss the pain. The crowd roars above me, a blur of sound, but it fades into the background, just white noise against the primal scream of agony from within. I push through the next play, forcing my body to obey, to skate, to fight for the puck as if nothing's wrong, as if every cell in my shoulder isn't shrieking for me to stop.

From the corner of my eye, I catch Lexi on the sidelines. She's too sharp, too keen, seeing through the façade I'm desperately maintaining. There's worry there, mixed with that no-nonsense edge she wields like her own personal hockey stick—ready to knock some sense into anyone who crosses her path.

She knows. Damn it. But acknowledging her silent alarm would make this real, and I can't have that—not now, not when we're neck and neck with the clock ticking down. I'm not Noah, ready to go moon-eyed and yes-ma'am the second I stub a toe. So I do what I do best: ignore the pain, ignore her concern, and pour every last bit of defiance I possess into the game.

The whistle blows, signaling a timeout. I coast to our bench, gripping the top of the boards for support, every labored breath punctuated by a jolt of pain from my shoulder. I'm fine. Gotta be fine.

"Hey, Wes."

I glance up to find Lexi leaning over the barrier, ponytail swaying, her eyes reflecting the arena lights and something else...concern maybe? She's ditched her clipboard for a more hands-on approach, it seems.

"Let me check out that shoulder," she says, her voice low and serious beneath the cacophony of fans seeking blood or glory—whichever comes first. "Or Drew can."

"Lexi, I'm good," I insist, trying to infuse confidence into my words, to sound convincing enough that maybe I'll believe it myself. "Just a little tweak, nothing major."

She raises an eyebrow, clearly not buying the act. "Wes, you're holding your arm like it's about to fall off. At least let me tape it up or something."

"Really, I'm—" I start but stop short as a fresh wave of pain crashes through me when I move my arm. I grit my teeth and force a smile. "I appreciate it, but I can handle it."

"Stubborn much?" she snaps, crossing her arms—a mirror image of defiance to my own.

"Part of my charm," I shoot back, hoping the playful arrogance will deflect her attention.

"Fine," Lexi relents with a sigh, but her eyes don't leave mine. With a last look of reluctant acceptance, she steps back, blending into the sea of team jackets and posterboard signs.

The game won't wait for my shoulder to sort itself out. Drew doesn't know—I've managed to hide it from him, and he's luckily been busy because of Noah and a few freshmen who've taken hits. So I've slid under the radar. I wonder how long I'll be able to, especially with Lexi watching like a hawk.

I'm back on the ice, slicing through defenders like they're cones in a drill. My shoulder screams with each shift of my body, but I shove the pain into a dark corner of my mind. Focus. That's all I need. The crowd is a distant roar, the game a blur of motion and adrenaline. I can see Lexi in the stands, lips press into a thin line, and I can see the words she wants to hurl at me, each one a missile aimed straight at my stubbornness.

I push off, harder, faster, driven by the need to prove her wrong, to prove everyone wrong. My shoulder aches like a warning, but I drown it out with the roar of the crowd. It's just me, the ice, and the puck. Everything else fades away. I focus on the puck, now a blur of black against the white ice as it dances between sticks, players jockeying for control. My breath comes out in foggy bursts.

"Jacobs! On your left!" The shout slices through the cacophony of cheers and skates carving ice.

I pivot, ignoring the sharp protest from my shoulder, and intercept a pass. I fake left, then right, a move that's second nature, except this time my shoulder doesn't quite follow through. The pain is a hot wire, coiling tighter with every maneuver. Gritting my teeth, I barrel forward, willing myself not to wince or falter under the scrutiny of fans and foes alike.

There's an opening—I see it, a clear shot to the goal. With every stride, I gather speed, the crowd's anticipation amplifying my own. This is it, the moment to silence doubts, to silence *her*. But as I wind up for the shot, muscles tensed and ready, something's off.

My arm feels like it's moving through molasses, heavy and uncooperative. The puck rockets off my stick, but the trajectory's all wrong. It sails wide, slamming into the boards with a hollow thud that echoes my own frustration. The groan from the crowd is audible, a collective sigh that mirrors the sinking feeling in my gut.

"Focus, Jacobs!" That's the coach's voice, gruff and edged with concern. But focus isn't so easy when every shift feels like you're dragging an anchor.

I take up position again, watching as the play shifts back to our zone. I'm there, always there, ready to battle for possession, to do what's necessary for the team. But the movements that used to be fluid are now staccato, jagged edges where smooth lines should be. I manage a decent check, more out of sheer force of will than actual physical prowess, and we regain control of the puck.

"Pass it!" someone yells, and I comply, sending the puck spinning down the ice. But even that simple action sends tremors of pain radiating through my arm. My passes lack their usual sniper precision; they're good enough, sure, but anyone who really knows hockey can tell—the edge, my edge, is dulled.

"Keep your head up, Wes!" I can hear Lexi's voice in my head, part chastisement, part worry. I push it aside, along with the twinge of guilt for brushing her off earlier. There's no room for either on the ice.

Play after play, I'm there, present in body if not entirely in capability. The grit that got me here, from those Minneapolis rinks to college glory, fuels me, but it's clear that something's amiss. I refuse to look at Lexi, stationed by the bench with her kit of tapes and ice packs, her eyes likely analyzing my every compromised move.

"Time!" I call out, tapping my stick against the ice as the period winds down. I skate toward the bench. The whistle shrieks, signaling the intermission, and I finally allow myself a grimace as I slump onto the bench.

"Good hustle, Wes," one of my teammates claps me on the back, oblivious to how much that 'good hustle' is costing me. I nod, chest heaving, sweat mingling with the cold air. I'm running on fumes and stubborn pride, and even I have to wonder—how long before one or both run out?

We're back in before I feel ready. The puck glides across the ice, a tantalizing promise of victory that my body screams to chase. I will it to come closer, to meet the blade of my stick with the grace and force I'm known for. But as I surge forward, shoulder throbbing, there's a hitch in my stride, a betrayal by my own flesh and bone.

"Jacobs! Eyes on the puck!" Coach bellows from the sidelines, his voice a piercing drill through the cacophony of the arena. He doesn't know the half of it—that each shift feels like skating through wet cement with a boulder strapped to my back.

I grit my teeth, trying to focus on the game, but my shoulder screams louder than the roar of the crowd. The pain is a white-hot line of fire, spreading from my clavicle down to my fingertips. It's not just discomfort now; it's a warning siren I've been ignoring for too long.

A rookie mistake, some might say. And they'd be right. Because pride has me by the throat, and it's choking the sense out of me. Lexi's words echo in my mind. Maybe—just maybe—I should have listened.

"Jacobs, what are you doing?" Noah's voice cuts through, laced with annoyance. "You're off your game, man."

I want to snap at him, throw back something witty and biting. But the energy it would take... I don't have it to spare. Not anymore.

I'm playing more on instinct than skill. Each pass is a gamble, each shot a prayer. The opposing team's winger barrels toward me, and I brace for impact, knowing this might be the straw that breaks the camel's back—or the shoulder.

"Crap," I hiss as I dodge the hit at the last second. The sharp pivot sends a jolt up my arm. It's a humbling thing, realizing your limits. Mine are shouting at me, loud and clear, and as the period comes to a close, I glide off the ice, my arm hanging uselessly by my side. There's no shaking it off this time. No, pretending that I'm fine when every cell in my body is rebelling against the facade.

Drew and Lexi are there the second I'm off the rink. Drew's eyes are pinched. He looks a little pissed.

"Drew—" I start, "It's nothing."

He jerks his head toward a nearby bench, and I sit.

"Let me look at it." Lexi's voice is soft but insistent, a lifeline thrown into the turbulent sea of my stubbornness.

I lock gazes with her, and something inside me shifts. Maybe it's the pain, maybe it's the exhaustion, or maybe I'm just tired of being my own worst enemy.

"All right," I breathe out, the word tasting like defeat but feeling strangely like relief. "All right, Lexi."

Her hand reaches out, steady and sure, and I know that whatever happens next is going to change the game entirely. But as her fingers gently probe the area around my shoulder, testing its movement and making me wince, I realize that this isn't just about hockey anymore.

It's about trust, about letting someone in—someone who might just see through the cracks in my armor.

CHAPTER FOUR: LEXI

The final buzzer blares, slicing through the electric current of anticipation that's been buzzing in my veins. I leap to my feet, joining the thunderous applause and cheers that ricochet off the arena walls. My heart races like I've been the one on the ice, dodging checks and firing pucks, not just an observer—an anxious one. The players swarm the goalie, a tangle of jerseys, sticks hoisted in victorious salute. And there, among them, are the guys I've taped up, iced down, and who have pushed themselves to their limits. Pride swells in my chest, warm and effervescent, as if their win is partly mine.

"Way to go!" I holler, though my voice is just a drop in the ocean of celebration. The energy is palpable, the joy uncontainable, and it's impossible not to feel connected to every player out there.

Or concerned—especially about Wes, who's been benched since Drew convinced him that his shoulder needs help. That continuing risked permanent damage.

He hadn't been happy.

We funnel out of the stands, a human river surging toward the after-party. It's not long until we're all at the local watering hole, The Draft. The scent of victory is sweet, mingled with the sharp tang of sweat and the beer that's already flowing freely. Strobe lights pulse, syncopated with the bass thumping from the speakers, turning the room into a living organism, throbbing with life. The team, fans, and other locals all flood the space.

"Lexi! You made it!" Dean "The Machine" Hartley barrels toward me, his grin as wide as the goalpost.

"Wouldn't miss this for the world," I shout back, high-fiving him. It's nice to be included. The reluctance of these guys to accept me—the wariness, really—seems to be melting away. Dean hollers over at the rest of the team. Soon, we're engulfed in a sea of backslaps and bear hugs.

Laughter bubbles up from deep within, mingling with the shouts and music. I'm jostled gently from side to side, the rhythm instinctive, shoulder to shoulder with friends, teammates, and fellow supporters who've ridden the rollercoaster of the season together.

"Drink?" someone offers, and I accept a pint of foamy beer, the froth tickling my nose as I take a cautious sip. It's lukewarm and slightly bitter, but tonight, it might as well be champagne.

Around me, the party undulates. People clink cups, exchange stories louder than necessary over the music, and replay the game's highlights with grandiose gestures. There's an infectious camaraderie in the air, the kind that can only be forged on the ice and fueled by shared triumphs.

"Dean, that check in the second period was epic," I yell over the music, my lips close to his ear so he can hear me. He throws his head back and laughs, the sound rich and carefree. "Had to make sure they knew we weren't playing around," he boasts, his eyes twinkling with mischief.

I weave through the throng of revelers, my pulse still racing from the game's final buzzer. The team's victory is fresh, a zesty tang on my tongue like the citrus punch I snag from the bartender to replace the beer. It tastes much better—but the beer has already lightened my spirits. My laughter dances with the pop tracks blaring from speakers that are working overtime tonight.

"Lexi! Over here!" someone calls, and I swivel, scanning the crowd for the familiar voice.

"Great game, Aces!" another fan shouts as I squeeze past, nodding appreciatively.

"Couldn't have done it without Wes's goal," I shout back, but even as I say it, the taste in my mouth turns bittersweet.

Wes. Wes Jacobs—the very name seems to skate along the edge of my patience. It's not just his cavalier attitude or how he takes every rule as a mere suggestion. No, it's deeper than that. It's the way he pushes boundaries, both on the ice and off, especially with me.

"Speak of the devil," I mutter under my breath as I spot him across the room, surrounded by a group of fans clamoring for his attention. He's all charm and easy smiles, his laugh low and hypnotic. But I know better. I've seen the strain around his eyes when he thinks no one's looking—when the adrenaline fades and pain seeps through the cracks of his facade. He said real athletes grin and bear it, but I know that's asking for trouble.

"Hey, Wes," Dean calls out, slinging an arm around my shoulders, "Did you see that final shot I made? The one that won us the game?"

Wes's gaze flits in my direction, and our eyes lock—a silent clash of wills. His smile doesn't reach his eyes this time. "Not now, Dean," he says, deflecting with a shrug that looks more calculated than casual. He turns his attention to the gaggle in front of him, who I notice are all giggling coeds.

"Don't want to congratulate your teammates?" I chide, the words slipping out before I can stop them. I'm teasing, but there's an edge to my voice that I can't quite cloak.

He rolls his shoulder, a subtle motion, but I catch it. "No need to lecture, Turner," Wes retorts, his tone light but sharp as skates on ice.

"Wouldn't dream of it," I shoot back, my own smile feeling forced.

Dean's grip on my shoulder tightens momentarily, and I realize he's trying to keep the peace. We're supposed to be celebrating, not picking at scabs. I make my escape under the pretense of refilling my drink, leaving Wes and his entourage behind.

But fate, it seems, isn't on my side. As I round a corner, navigating away from the boisterous heart of the party, I bump right into the man himself—Wes, sans his admirers, his eyes dark and intense.

"Trying to provoke me, Turner?" he asks, quirking an eyebrow.

"I wouldn't waste the time," I retort, meeting his gaze squarely.

For a moment, we simply stand there, the sounds of the party dimmed by distance, the air between us charged with unsaid words and unresolved tension. Finally, I crack.

"Your shoulder," I begin, unable to hold back, "you need to rest it."

"Lexi, Coach cleared me," he counters, his jaw setting in that stubborn line I've come to recognize and dread.

"Coach? Not Drew? That doesn't mean you're a hundred percent. You can't just—" I cut myself off, aware that raising my concerns might only drive him further into denial. And as an intern, I can only push so much. If I overstep, I could lose my internship. And that looks bad, both to any hope of a future career, let alone finding a new place to get my hands-on hours if the Aces boot me.

"Can't just what? Play? Do my job?" Wes's voice rises, and I bristle at his defensive tone.

"Look, I'm not your enemy here," I say, exasperated. "Just because you can play through the pain doesn't mean you should."

"Thanks for the advice, *Doc*," he replies, sarcasm lacing his words, "but I'll take my chances."

We're locked in a standoff, neither willing to yield, our mutual stubbornness keeping us rooted to the spot. It's a dance we've perfected over time—one step forward, two steps back. And yet, despite the irritation simmering between us, I can't fully tamp down the inexplicable pull I feel toward him.

"Listen to me, Wes," I say, my voice low and taut with frustration. "You're not invincible. That shoulder needs rest, not another round on the ice."

"Rest?" He scoffs, a flash of anger in those piercing blue eyes. "There's no time for rest, Lexi. We're on the brink of playoffs. I can't just sit out."

"Can't or won't?" I challenge, stepping closer, invading his space as much as he's invaded mine. "Because it seems to me you're confusing stubbornness with strength."

"Maybe I am," he snaps back, his proximity setting off a different kind of spark within me, one that has no place here. "But I know my limits better than anyone—better than you."

"Your limits?" The incredulity is clear as day in my tone. "Wes, your macho act might fool the fans, but I know what playing through this could mean for your career—"

His laugh is bitter, slicing through the tension. "What do you know about my career, huh? You think because you've read some textbooks, you get it? This is my life. Hockey is all I've got."

"Exactly!" My hands are animated now, slicing through the air between us like the sharp edge of a skate. "It's your life, Wes. And if you blow out your shoulder for good, what then?"

"Then at least I went down swinging." His jaw clenches, a muscle ticking in his cheek, betraying the pain he's too proud to admit. "Not everyone has the luxury of backup plans, Lexi. Not all of us have led cushy little legacy lives."

"Fine," I snap, turning on my heel, "do what you want, Wes. It's not like you ever listen anyway."

As I walk away, the music and laughter swell behind me, but the festive atmosphere feels miles away. Our argument hangs suspended in the air, unresolved and raw, a crackling undercurrent beneath the surface of celebration. The afterparty's buzz thrums through me, a cocktail of victory and adrenaline. My heart races, not just from the high of our win but from the brewing storm I've walked away from. Wes Jacobs, with his infuriating smugness and penchant for self-destruction, is a hurricane I'm perpetually drawn to—but not sure I have the strength to weather.

A storm that follows me out into the night air, where I had hoped for some solace, some cooling-off. He catches up to me a minute after I enter the side alley by the bar, the clang of the metal door slamming open against the building announcing his arrival.

"Why are you being such a damned…complication?" he grinds out, running a hand through his jet-black hair.

"Complication?" I echo, my pulse hammering at the admission. But I can't afford to focus on the heat that word ignites within me, not when there's so much more at stake. "If that's what it takes for you to listen, then I'll be the biggest damn complication you've ever had to deal with."

He looks at me then, really looks at me, and for a fleeting moment, I see the vulnerability he's so adept at hiding. Even as I stand my ground, my chest tightens, knowing that this fight is bigger than just a stubborn athlete and a concerned medic. It's about two people caught in a dangerous dance, one where every step could lead either to salvation or ruin.

"Fight all you want, Turner," he says with a wry twist of his lips that doesn't reach his eyes. "But I'm not the type to back down."

"Neither am I," I fire back, my resolve as unyielding as the ice beneath our feet. I jab a finger toward his chest, my breath coming out in quick puffs of frustration. "You think you're invincible, don't you? That nothing can touch Wes Jacobs, the star forward?"

His jaw clenches, and he grabs my wrist gently but firmly, lowering my hand away from him. "Invincible? No. Determined? Hell, yes."

"Stubborn, you mean," I retort.

"God, you're infuriating!" Wes explodes, running a hand through his jet-black hair. "Do you think I do this because I like pain? Because I don't care if I end up broken? I have to play—it's all I've got."

"And what about after hockey, Wes?" I demand, stepping closer. "What happens when the one thing you've got leaves you with nothing but regret and a lifetime of 'what ifs'?"

He scoffs, shaking his head as if trying to dispel my words like an annoying buzz around his ears. "You think you have all the answers, don't you, Turner? Just because you've seen a few injuries, you think you know my future?"

"Better than you apparently!" My hands ball into fists at my sides, my nails digging into my palms. The energy between us is almost palpable, every word we hurl carving deeper into the core of what's really at stake here: not just a shoulder, but dreams, fears, and the undeniable tension that's been building.

"Fine! Ignore the advice!" I throw my hands up in exasperation. "Ignore the fact that I actually care what happens to you."

"Is that what you want?" Wes steps forward, closing the gap until we're only inches apart. "For me to ignore you?"

"Maybe I do," I say, though my heart races at his proximity.

"Lexi..." His voice softens, and for a moment, I see the vulnerability he usually keeps hidden beneath layers of defiance and bravado.

"Then maybe you should ignore me," he says quietly. But there's a new tension in the air, an unsaid challenge that hangs heavy between us.

My breath catches as he reaches up, brushing a stray lock of hair from my face. His hand trails down, settling at the nape of my neck as he gently pulls me closer. For a moment, our gazes lock, his ice-blue eyes searching mine, reflecting a tumultuous mixture of anger, frustration, and something else. Something raw and unnamed that sends a shiver down my spine.

"Wes..." My voice comes out in a barely audible whisper.

And then he's kissing me. It's angry and desperate, a testament to the storm that has been brewing between us from the very start. His hands tighten in my hair as his mouth moves over mine, each press a challenge, a promise, a plea. Somewhere in the back of my mind, I know I should push him away. But the feel of him, the taste of him—it's a balm to the turmoil inside me. I surrender to the kiss, allowing myself this one moment of weakness.

Eventually, he pulls back, his breath hitching as he rests his forehead against mine. "Do you still want me to ignore you?" he murmurs against my lips.

I swallow hard, looking into his eyes, now soft and uncertain. "I... I don't know," I admit, my voice barely a whisper.

"Lexi," he breathes out, his thumb stroking my cheek softly. "No matter how infuriating you are, or how much we argue...there's something between us, and you can't deny it."

His words hang heavy in the air. My heart thuds painfully in my chest, my mind warring with what I know is right and what I feel. With a sigh, I pull away from him slightly, my eyes averted. I need space, space to breathe, to think, to process all of these overwhelming emotions.

Before he can say anything else, a cheer erupts from inside the bar, drawing our attention momentarily.

"Sounds like your teammates could use some supervision," I point out, grateful for the distraction.

"Looks like you could use another drink," Wes counters, and there's an edge to his words that tells me we're not done—not by a long shot.

"Maybe it's a bad idea to mix business with pleasure," I say, my voice steady even though my heart isn't.

"Who's talking about business?" he murmurs, leaning in again, so close I can feel his breath on my cheek. "This could be all pleasure, Turner."

And just like that, the tension is back, coiling tight in my stomach. I want to push him away, to erase the smudge his presence leaves on my composure, but instead, I stand my ground. Because Lexi Turner doesn't back down—not from hockey players with egos as bruised as their shoulders, and certainly not from her own confusing desires.

"Maybe for you," I manage to say. "But for me, this" —I gesture between us— "is just another game. And I'm not playing."

"Yet," he adds, his gaze locked on mine.

"Yet," I echo, and then I turn and bolt for the back door, feeling like I've just made a promise I have no intention of keeping.

CHAPTER FIVE: LEXI

As I step onto the campus, the embrace of winter surrounds me completely. The air is crisp, tinged with the frosty bite that only a northern winter can deliver, and the crunch of snow underfoot marks each step with a satisfying punctuation. I'm on my way to an immersion observation, and I'm looking forward to it.

Trees, stripped of their foliage, wear a delicate coating of snow, their branches creating stark silhouettes against a pale gray sky. I walk along the winding paths that ribbon through the campus, bordered by an expanse of immaculately groomed lawns now transformed into endless white sheets. It's early in the morning, and the snow is undisturbed except for the occasional tracks of rabbits and squirrels. The tranquility of the scene is punctuated only by the distant sound of the campus bell tower chiming the hour, its notes seeming crisper, carried further by the cold air.

The buildings around me range from historic, ivy-covered halls to modern structures of glass and steel. The older buildings, with their sturdy brick facades and large windows, seem to hold within them the warmth of decades of bustling academic life. Their roofs are frosted with snow, with icicles dangling from the eaves, sparkling in the occasional sunlight that breaks through the clouds.

As I pass by these academic halls, I can see inside where students are already gathering, some bundled up in scarves and beanies, cradling steaming cups of coffee or hot chocolate. The glow of warm light from the classrooms promises a refuge from the chilly outdoors, and laughter spills out every time someone opens a door, a brief blast of warm air following them out into the cold.

The heart of the campus is the student union, a bustling hub of activity. Even now, in the depths of winter, it draws students like a warm hearth. Inside, the atmosphere is lively. Groups of students sit around tables, some studying, others just chatting and enjoying themselves before classes. The scent of baked goods and coffee fills the air, mingling with the dampness of snow-trodden coats and winter boots left to dry by the door.

Across the way is the campus library, an impressive edifice of stone with tall, arched windows. It stands like a sentinel over the campus, its quiet dignity undisturbed by the weather. Inside, the library is a sanctuary of silence and study. Rows of books tower from floor to ceiling, their spines offering a spectrum of knowledge spanning centuries. Students sit at scattered tables, lost in thought or deep in study, the only sounds the soft murmur of whispered discussions and the occasional rustling of pages being turned.

Further down, the athletic fields lie dormant under a thick blanket of snow, the usual vibrant greens replaced by the stark whites and grays of winter. The tracks are barely visible, and the football field looks like a vast, empty canvas. Yet, the promise of spring hangs in the air, a silent understanding that this sleeping giant will awaken with the return of warmth.

This college, with its blend of tradition and modernity, offers more than just a place for academic pursuit. It provides a sense of community and belonging, a space where warmth is found not only in heated buildings but in the connections forged over shared experiences of enduring and embracing the bitter cold together. And the cold isn't something I can escape—it's waiting for me as I round the corner to the hockey arena, waiting for me to come try to conquer the ice.

Or, at least help my players to.

***

I lace up my boots with a determined pull, the leather straps pressing into my fingers, grounding me. The crisp snap of each eyelet is a tiny battle cry, echoing the tug-of-war in my chest. With one final tug on my laces, I'm ready. I push through the double doors of the arena, the air immediately biting at my cheeks. It's familiar and comforting—the scent of freshly Zamboni-ed ice mingling with the sharp tang of sweat and determination. My father used to say arenas hold the spirit of every game played within their walls. If that's true, this place is a cathedral.

"Turner!" someone shouts—a greeting or a warning, I can't tell.

"Present!" I call back, injecting as much cheer into the word as I can muster. Today, I'm all business—Lexi Turner, intern extraordinaire, soon-to-be savior of athletes' careers. No tangled emotions allowed. I'm practicing with the team in order to observe them on-ice, up close and personal.

Too bad I can't stop thinking about how up close and personal Wes Jacobs and I got last night. The rink unfolds before me, a glacial stretch of pristine white. Players glide across it, their movements the embodiment of power and grace, a dance of giants clad in padding and steel blades. As I watch them, the energy is palpable—the raw, kinetic promise of competition, of camaraderie, of victory and defeat told in sweeps of stick against puck.

"Hey, Turner! Eyes on the prize!" Dean "The Machine" Hartley calls out as he zips past, somehow making his burly frame pirouette on the ice in a mockery of figure skating.

"Keep your day job, Hartley!" I retort, not missing a beat.

"Ouch," he laughs, slapping a hand over his heart but grinning wide.

There's work to be done, and I'm here to do it. Ankles flexing in my sturdy boots, I stride toward the team benches, clipboard in hand. My job is clear—keep these athletes in top form, manage injuries with precision and care, and above all, maintain professional distance. But as the cold seeps through my jacket, chilling me to the bone, I can't help but feel the heat of two particular gazes: Noah's warming like a gentle hearth fire, Wes's sparking like flint on steel.

Wes kissed me, but I didn't miss how Noah's eyes held more than professional interest when I was tending to his ankle.

My lips twitch into a smile at Dean's retreating figure; the banter is part of the gig, a language all its own in the rink. But there's no time to dwell on the jester of the ice, nor on Noah and Wes. My gaze shifts, scanning for the next task, the next player's movement—but instead, it catches snippets of conversation floating from the cluster of bodies by the boards.

"Can't wait for that cabin retreat, man. It's gonna be epic," one of them chuckles, slinging his arm over another's shoulder.

"Totally. Just hope the rookies don't get too wild," another responds, the laughter in his voice reaching me across the distance.

A cabin retreat. The thought sends a ripple through me, both thrilling and unsettling. Noah, Wes, the entire team—trapped in the wilderness together. It'll be tight quarters, shared spaces... and far too much opportunity for the emotions I'm wrestling with to surface. My mind wanders to snowy hikes, late-night campfires, and the inevitable proximity to Noah and Wes.

"Hey, Lexi, you coming on the retreat this weekend?" The voice breaks through my reverie, and I look up to find Noah's warm brown eyes on me, concern etched in the lines around them.

"Wouldn't miss it," I reply, maybe more curtly than I intend. But the smile he gives me is kind, forgiving.

More like Drew said it would count for intern hours, I think.

Not that I don't want the experience, but these "team retreats" are often no more than a getaway party weekend for the team to blow off steam.

"Great! We could use your expertise out there. And..." He hesitates, a rare vulnerability flickering in his gaze. "It'll be nice to have you around."

"Thanks, Noah. I'll make sure to pack my professional hat—or should I say helmet?" I joke, trying to shake off the flutter his words cause in my chest.

"Helmet might be safer," he agrees, his smile broadening before he turns back to the others, leaving me with a heart that's suddenly beating double-time.

"Safer indeed," I whisper to the empty air, knowing full well that no helmet in the world could protect me from the collision course of feelings hurtling my way.

***

Before I can blink, Saturday morning comes. I'm elbow-deep in athletic tape and gauze pads, trying to find the delicate balance between thoroughness and efficiency. It's a tetris game of medical supplies as I slot ice packs next to compression braces, ensuring everything is packed tightly into the kit. The air in the equipment room is charged with an anticipatory buzz, everyone moving with purpose, laughter echoing off the walls as they toss gear bags into the pile.

"Lexi, you reckon we'll need this many splints?" Dean jests, holding up an armful of aluminum strips that glint under the fluorescent lights.

"Drew said plan ahead. And considering your track record on the ice, I'd pack double," I shoot back without missing a beat, and a round of chuckles ripples through the room.

"Ouch, our very own PT's got jokes," Dean smirks, but there's respect there too. He knows I'm not just here for laughs—I'm here to keep them all in one piece.

"All right, team, let's get those bags loaded up!" Noah's voice cuts above the din, authoritative yet warm. Everyone hops to it, hefting duffel bags over shoulders, boxes of snacks under arms. I grab a cooler filled to the brim with hydration drinks and follow the human caravan out toward the bus. As I step outside, a sudden hush blankets the world, the kind only a first snowfall can bring. Snowflakes drift lazily from the gray expanse above, dotting my eyelashes and melting on my cheeks. I pause, letting the cooler rest at my feet, and tilt my head back, mesmerized by the dance of countless tiny ice crystals.

"Hey, Lexi, catch!" A voice pulls me from the trance, and instinctively, I look forward just in time to see a snowball explode against my chest. Laughter erupts around me, and I brush off the wet patches, grinning despite myself. The source of the attack makes my chest pinch—Wes, grinning and handsome.

"Real mature, guys!" But I can't suppress the warmth spreading through me, not from the cold, but from the light-hearted mischief and the unbidden memory of Wes's kiss.

"Come on, before we turn into popsicles," Wes calls out, his teasing tone not quite masking the heat in his eyes. He reaches out, offering a hand to help with the cooler, and for a moment, I'm caught in the crossfire of his electric blue gaze.

"Thanks," I say, shaking off the snowflakes—and the flutter in my stomach—as we make our way to the bus. The beauty of the early winter tableau etches itself into my memory: the sharp contrast of red and gold leaves blanketed in white, the muffled sounds of the city, and the team's laughter as we embark on this adventure together.

There's something about the first real snowfall that always gets me—it's the promise of newness, of wiping the slate clean and starting over. Even the familiar outside grounds of the arena look magical, transformed into a scene straight out of those cheesy holiday movies I claim to hate but secretly love.

I tug my beanie down further over my ears and shove my hands deeper into the pockets of my jacket. Can't get too sentimental; it's cold enough to freeze your nose hairs. My gaze drifts across the parking lot as more players start to emerge from the building, their voices loud against the quiet snowscape. They're clustered together, laughing and shoving each other playfully, the very picture of camaraderie.

"Looks like it's gonna be a memorable weekend," Wes remarks, a hint of something unreadable in his voice.

"Definitely," I agree, feeling the weight of anticipation settle in.

The bus is warm compared to the bite of the autumn air, a little haven on wheels ready to whisk us away to the cabin retreat. I find a seat near the front, dropping my duffel bag onto it before helping others stow their gear in the overhead compartments. Everyone's buzzing with energy, the excitement palpable as we settle in for the drive. Thankfully, Wes takes a seat at the back of the bus.

I slide into my mid-level seat, pull my phone out for one last check—zero messages, which is both a relief and a tiny stab of disappointment—and then turn it off. This weekend is about being present, about building connections with the team, and maybe figuring out what my heart wants along the way. A tricky game plan, but I've always been up for a challenge.

"Ready for some forced bonding?" Noah teases from the seat behind me, leaning forward so his breath tickles the back of my neck.

"Only if it involves marshmallows and ghost stories," I shoot back without missing a beat. The corners of his lips tug upward, and I can feel the smile more than see it.

"Scared you'll be stuck between me and Wes by the campfire?" he whispers conspiratorially.

"Please, I'd need to be scared of you two first," I retort, though my heartbeat betrays the casual facade.

As the bus engine rumbles to life and we pull away from the curb, I allow myself a contented sigh. The snow continues to fall gently outside, the landscape passing by in a blur of white and gray. I'm cocooned in this moving bubble with a bunch of rowdy hockey players, speeding toward an unknown that's both thrilling and terrifying.

But right now, with the hum of anticipation in the air and the promise of adventure ahead, I wouldn't have it any other way. Bring on the cabin retreat.

CHAPTER SIX: NOAH

My heart's a jackhammer in my chest as I stare at the rugged cabin nestled between towering pines, its cozy amber lights winking through the dusk. The retreat is finally here, the one weekend where the entire hockey team shacks up in the wilderness to bond and blow off steam. But it's not the promise of beers by the bonfire or late-night poker that's got my pulse racing—it's Lexi. God, just thinking about her sends a jolt of electricity through my veins.

"Move it, Captain!" Dean yells from behind, snapping me out of my reverie. I grab my duffle bag with a grin and make my way to the cabin, the crunch of snow and gravel underfoot syncing with the beat of my anticipation. This isn't just any retreat; it's the perfect chance to spend some real time with Lexi away from the rink, the gym, and the endless grind of classes.

We pour into the cabin like a flood, laughter and chatter echoing off the log walls. Someone cranks up the tunes, and the place comes alive with the kind of energy only a bunch of college athletes can muster. Dean wastes no time challenging half the guys to a game of foosball, his competitive streak a blazing fire even off the ice.

"First round's on the losers!" he hollers, and the room erupts in cheers and trash talk.

I dodge a flying ping-pong ball—it looks like Wes has already started an epic table tennis tournament—and find myself grinning. This is our world, a brotherhood forged on sweat and steel blades. And yet, amidst the shouts and high-fives, there's a corner of my mind that's solely reserved for Lexi.

I glance around, searching for a glimpse of sandy blonde hair tied back in a practical ponytail, or those eyes that seem to see right through me. She's here somewhere, I'm sure of it, and the thought alone fuels my eagerness to join in on the festivities.

"Hey, Bishop, you in?" Wes calls out, waving a paddle. "Or are you too scared to face my wicked backhand?"

"I'd be more worried about your forehand if it actually hit the table," I shoot back, accepting the challenge with a smirk. I wonder, though, about his shoulder. There's no sign of Wes being in pain—but he's good at hiding it.

As the night wears on, the air thick with warmth from the crackling fireplace, I find my gaze wandering back to Lexi. Each time our eyes meet, there's a flicker of something unspoken, a shared secret that neither of us has voiced. Her laughter rings out, genuine and untamed, and it's like a siren song, pulling me into her orbit without fail.

I catch another glance, a silent conversation in a room full of noise. She looks away quickly, cheeks flushed from the heat or maybe from the rush of whatever this is between us. I can't help but smile, knowing the feeling all too well. There's an undeniable energy in these stolen moments, a teasing promise of what's to come. This isn't just about hockey anymore—as the evening unfolds, I'm already strategizing my next move, because when it comes to Lexi Turner, I'm determined to win more than just a game. The bass of a familiar ballad vibrates through the wooden floorboards as someone commandeers the playlist, shifting the cabin's energy from raucous to reflective. I feel my pulse sync with the rhythm—a slow, deliberate thud that echoes my rising nerves.

"Looks like the universe is throwing me a sign," I say, sidling up next to her where she stands at the sliding glass doors that lead to the back deck, my voice barely audible over the music. Lexi turns, her gaze meeting mine, and I see a question in them, one that mirrors my own hesitation.

"Or maybe it's just a playlist," she counters, but there's a playful tilt to her lips that tells me she's game for whatever I'm suggesting.

I let out a breath I didn't know I was holding and close the distance between us. "Dance with me, Lexi?" The words come out more like a hopeful whisper than the confident invitation I intended.

For a heart-stopping moment, she doesn't move, and I brace myself for rejection. But then, surprise flickers across her face, softening into something warmer. She sets down her drink, her hand reaching out to mine. Her touch is steady, grounding, as if she's the one comforting me instead of the other way around.

"Sure, Captain," she says, her tone teasing, but there's a gentleness in the way she lets me lead her to the center of the room—a clearing made by teammates who've brought their own romantic partners on the party weekend. The room seems paused mid-conversation, the rest of the group's attention drawn to the unexpected pair taking the floor. As we step into the crowd's makeshift circle, I'm acutely aware of every point where our bodies are close but not touching. The hand resting lightly on her waist, her fingers curled around mine—each point of contact is like a live wire, sending a jolt straight to my core.

"Didn't take you for the dancing type," Lexi murmurs, a hint of curiosity in her gaze as she falls into step with me.

"Full of surprises," I shoot back with a grin, hoping it masks the thunderous beating of my heart. It's just a dance, I tell myself. One song in a retreat meant to build team spirit. Except, as we sway gently to the music, it feels like anything but 'just a dance.'

The world shrinks to the size of this room, to the space we occupy. A soft melody wraps around us, a gentle caress as intoxicating as a fine wine, and Lexi and I fall into a rhythm that feels as natural as breathing. Our bodies move in perfect harmony, swaying to the subtle ebb and flow of the music, our feet finding their places in an unspoken agreement.

Her gaze holds mine, green eyes bright with an emotion I can't quite name but am desperate to explore. It's as if the very air between us is charged, every other soul in this cabin retreat fading into nothingness. We're alone in the midst of laughter and chatter, two people moving as one in a dance that's less about steps and more about the silent conversation we're having with our eyes.

"Didn't peg you for someone who could actually keep up," Lexi teases, her voice barely above the whisper of violins in the background. Her tone is light, but there's a touch of sincerity there that tells me she's pleasantly surprised—not just by my dancing skills but by the ease between us.

"Guess you don't know everything about me, Turner," I retort playfully, but the truth is, I'm just as shocked at how right this feels. The way her body fits against mine, it's like finding a missing piece I didn't even know I was looking for.

A shiver runs through Lexi as my hand shifts slightly on the small of her back, fingers splayed over the fabric of her shirt. It's tentative, respectful, but undeniably possessive—a declaration without words that she's the only one I want to be holding right now. And when she leans into the touch, it's like confirmation that she doesn't mind being claimed. Heat blossoms in my chest, spreading warmth throughout my limbs. This feeling, having Lexi close, her body pressed to mine as we move to the music—it's something unfamiliar, yet overwhelmingly comforting. She's strong in my arms, her athletic build a testament to her passion for sports, yet there's a softness to her that contradicts the steel I've seen her wield against doubters and naysayers.

"Comfortable?" I ask, but the question sounds foolish even to my ears. How could she not be? I feel like I've been made to hold her, the contours of her body aligning with mine in a way that feels predestined.

"Surprisingly so," she admits, and the corner of her mouth quirks up in a smile that's reserved just for moments like this—genuine, unguarded, shared between just the two of us.

As we continue to dance, I realize this isn't just a momentary reprieve from the chaos of college life or the intense pressure of leading a hockey team to victory. This is a revelation—a realization that Lexi Turner isn't just a challenge to be met or a teammate to be respected. She's quickly becoming the highlight of every day, the reason my heart races with anticipation at the thought of what's to come.

I lean in closer to Lexi, the rhythm of the song setting a gentle pace for our bodies and our confessions. "When I was seven," I whisper against her ear, my breath mingling with the strands of her hair, "I used to dream about flying—not just on the ice, but literally soaring above it all."

She giggles softly, her breath warm on my neck. "Superhero complex much?"

"More like a superhuman wish," I counter, feeling the vibration of her laughter through our close contact. "Your turn. Any childhood dreams you're willing to share with me?"

"Okay," she murmurs, her voice a delicate hush, drawing me in more than any loud declaration could. "I wanted to be an astronaut—had this crazy fascination with the stars. And, well, you know, defying gravity."

"Defying gravity, huh?" I tease back, thinking how fitting it is for her, pushing limits on and off the ice.

"Absolutely," Lexi confirms, and there's a twinkle in her eye that tells me she's not just playing along; she means every word.

It's as if the rest of the retreat fades away, the noise and clamor of our teammates becoming a distant hum. The fairy lights strung across the wooden beams of the cabin ceiling cast a soft, ethereal glow around us, making Lexi's face seem even more captivating. Her eyes sparkle, reflecting the twinkling lights, and her smile—wide and unguarded—sends a jolt straight through me.

The song's final notes linger in the air, the melody winding down, signaling the end of our dance. But neither of us moves to break away. Our bodies remain close, the distance between our hearts nonexistent. I lower my forehead to rest against hers, and we breathe in unison, our gazes locked.

"Lexi," I start, the urgency in my voice betraying the surge of emotions I'm struggling to contain.

"Noah," she whispers back, the tone reflecting a world of possibilities.

In that prolonged moment, everything fades—the sounds of the cabin retreat, the shuffle of feet, the distant laughter. It's just Lexi and me, holding onto each other like we're the only two people left on earth, our hearts beating in harmony. The magic of the night wraps around us, tender and full of promise.

Then, ever so slowly, we begin to part, but the spell doesn't break. It lingers, tangible in the space between us, and I know that this dance—this moment—will replay in my mind long after the music has stopped. Stepping back into the whirlwind of the retreat, the heat of Lexi's palm lingers on my skin like a brand. Her laughter, mingled with those of our teammates, rings through the cabin, but it's as if I'm hearing everything from underwater. The memory of her in my arms is a vivid imprint in my mind, a reminder that something shifted between us tonight—a seismic shift that could change the very foundation of our dynamic.

I watch her meld back into the group seamlessly, her hair catching the light as she tilts her head back to laugh. There's an ease to her movements, a confidence that speaks volumes about who she is: Alexis Turner, a force to be reckoned with. But for those few minutes when we danced, she let me see past that.

My heart thrums with a cocktail of adrenaline and hope, the way it does before the final buzzer of a tied game. It's exhilarating, this feeling of being on the cusp of something monumental. As I lean against the wall, sipping a drink I don't remember grabbing, I can't tear my eyes away from her. She's unaware of the intensity of my stare, of how every quip that falls from her lips seems to be just for me, even when it's not.

"Hey there, Captain," Wes, my ever-observant winger, nudges me with his elbow, a knowing smirk on his face. "Looks like you left something out there on the dance floor."

"Maybe I did," I reply, unable to suppress the grin that tugs at my lips. The possibilities ahead seem infinite, and I'm ready to chase them down.

"What happened, did she bolt?" Wes teases with a raised eyebrow. "After that dance, I thought you'd be joined at the hip."

I shrug, feeling my cheeks heat just a little. What is it that I hear in Wes's voice? There's an edge that I can't identify. "It's not like that. It was just a dance."

"Sure, sure," he chuckles, clapping me on the shoulder a little too hard before he heads off to challenge someone to a game of darts.

I look over at Lexi. Despite the cold Minnesota air, something warm and undeniable has taken root between us, and I'm ready to tend to it, to see just how far it can grow. But is there something else that could stand in the way—and what does Wes have against my interest in the pretty new intern?

CHAPTER SEVEN: WES

I lean against the wooden wall of the cabin, a plastic cup of whatever punch the team decided to concoct clutched in my hand. My gaze drifts across the room, past the raucous laughter and drunken dance moves of my teammates, and lands on Lexi. She's dancing with Noah—Noah Bishop, our captain and Mr. Nice Guy himself. I take a swig from my cup, the liquid doing nothing to quench the heat rising in my chest.

There's something about the way her sandy blonde hair sways with each movement, the way her laugh reaches her eyes that makes it hard to look away. Jealousy and desire twist inside me like a Gordian knot. I should be out there, not Noah. But then again, I'm Wes Jacobs—the guy who rides the edge, never the one who gets the girl.

Lexi throws her head back, laughing at something Noah says, and I can't help but wonder what it would be like to be on the receiving end of that look. To be the one making her laugh. It's ridiculous, really, because up until this retreat, Lexi Turner was just another face in a crowd of college students. But now she's all sharp wit and confidence wrapped up in an athletic build that speaks volumes of her strength. Yeah, I've noticed. More than I should have.

"Hey, Jacobs, your slack-jawed gazing is creeping into stalker territory," Dean calls out, nudging my side as he passes by with a smirk.

"Shut it, Hartley," I mutter, pushing off the wall, determined to do something about this restless feeling clawing at me.

I sulk alone until I see her pull away from Noah—and I can't resist a momentary jab at *Captain Bishop* before I go to refill my drink. After, I stride over to where Lexi is now chatting with one of the defensemen, probably discussing some intricate play. My heart slams against my rib cage, but outwardly I'm calm—cool ice, just like on the rink. I catch her eye, and for a moment, it's like we're the only two people in the room.

"Lexi, can I talk to you? Outside?" My voice is steady, but there's an intensity there I don't bother to hide.

She looks at me, a hint of surprise flickering across her face, but she nods. "Sure, give me a sec."

"Actually," I say, the word cutting through the music, "now."

The defenseman raises his eyebrows but backs off without a word. The rest of the team is too caught up in their own revelries to notice us slipping out the front door. As I hold it open for her, Lexi brushes past me, and the faint scent of her perfume—a mix of something floral and the crisp winter air—hits me.

"Lead the way, Jacobs," she says, her voice laced with that ever-present sarcasm I can't get enough of.

I want to grin, to throw some cocky remark back at her, but instead, I simply nod and step into the night, knowing full well that this conversation could change everything.

Snow swirls around us as we step outside, a tempest of white cloaking the cabin retreat in a shroud of silent chaos. The frigid air bites at my cheeks, but it's nothing compared to the chill that's settled over me since seeing Lexi in Noah's arms. Flakes settle on her hair like a crown of winter, and I can't help but think she looks like some kind of ice princess—untouchable, ethereal.

"Wow, it's really coming down," she says, her breath forming clouds of mist as she turns her face toward the sky. "It's like being inside a snow globe."

"Except there's no shaking this," I reply, brushing off the snow that's already gathering on my shoulders.

We tread carefully along the path, the snow crunching beneath our boots. It's a sound that's usually comforting, synonymous with winter games and victory parties. But tonight, it's just the prelude to what I know needs to be said.

"Thanks for coming out here with me," I start, shoving my hands into my jacket pockets. I don't miss how it makes my shoulder twinge. Maybe I should lay off the ping-pong and darts. "I needed to get away from the noise for a bit."

"Is everything okay?" she asks, her expression sharp with concern, cutting through the falling snow and right into me.

I hesitate, watching the snowflakes dance between us. They're delicate things, unique and fleeting—kind of like moments, I guess. And this moment feels like one I won't get back if I don't seize it.

"Look, Lexi," I say, finally meeting her gaze. "This... all of this isn't easy for me. I'm not the guy who talks about feelings or opens up. But I've got these thoughts, these fears that I don't know how to handle."

"Everyone has fears, Wes. It's normal," she says softly, stepping closer. Her presence is like a fire—I shouldn't touch, but the warmth is tempting.

"Normal isn't something I'm familiar with," I admit with a forced chuckle. "I'm used to keeping people at a distance. Close is scary."

"Is that a good thing?" Her voice is barely above a whisper, yet it cuts through the howling wind.

"Depends on who you ask." My smile is wry. I glance down, watching the snow gather on the tips of her boots.

"Being scared isn't a weakness," she says, her hand finding mine, fingers intertwining. "Trust me, I know. It shows you care about something enough to worry about losing it."

The space between us shrinks, the way ice melts under a relentless sun. We're alone in this snow-clad world—just me, Lexi, and the silent dance of snowflakes around us. The cold bites at my cheeks, but her nearness is a bonfire I can't resist inching closer to.

"Your hands are freezing," she murmurs, her breath crystallizing in the air as it meets mine. Our eyes lock, and I'm entranced by the way her green irises catch the silver glow of the winter moon.

"Occupational hazard," I joke weakly, though humor seems out of place when every nerve-ending screams with the awareness of her. She's close enough that I catch the faint scent of her shampoo, something floral and undeniably Lexi, mingling with the fresh pine of the surrounding forest.

"Here," she says, stepping into the border of my personal space—a line long since blurred. She pulls our joined hands against her chest. The heat from her body seeps into my skin, and I fight back a shiver—not from the cold, but from the electric thrill of her touch.

"Better?" she asks, her voice softer now, laced with an undertone I dare not interpret. It's like we're skating on the same line, performing a duet where every synchronized move matters.

"Much," I admit, and it's the truth. The warmth isn't just physical; it's seeping into the cracks of my guarded heart, heating parts of me I didn't realize were frozen.

Her gaze flickers to my lips, then back to my eyes, and there's a question there—one I've been asking myself since the moment I realized the 'thing' between us wasn't just going to fade away. Since I kissed her at the bar. My thumb brushes against her knuckles, a silent answer to an unspoken query.

"Lexi..." Her name is a prayer I didn't know I was devout enough to offer, spoken with a reverence reserved for moments that change your course.

"Kiss me again, Wes," she whispers, a challenge wrapped in vulnerability. And who am I to deny either of us the inevitable?

The last remnants of distance vanish as I lean down, her face tilting up to meet mine. Our lips crash together in a kiss that ignites like a flare in the night, bright and all-consuming. There's no gentleness—it's all hunger and need and raw emotion pouring out after being dammed up for far too long.

Her arms wind around my neck, pulling me closer, while my hands find the small of her back, anchoring her to me as if she's the only solid thing in a world adrift. The snow continues to fall, dusting us in its silent witness to what feels like an earth-shattering connection.

Time loses meaning when you're tasting heaven, and that's what Lexi's lips feel like against mine—heaven, home, the damn winning goal in overtime. It's passion, it's fire, and it's terrifying in its intensity because kissing Lexi isn't just a kiss—it's a beginning, an admission, a surrender.

And as we break apart for air, panting and still so very close, I realize one kiss will never be enough. Not with her. Not now that I've had a taste of what's behind that stubborn sass and sharp wit. Lexi Turner, the girl who's managed to do the impossible—make Wes Jacobs want more than the thrill of the game.

She's my new adrenaline rush, my playoff season, and hell if I'm not ready to play for keeps. The world's gone white—snow swirling in a frenzied dance that blots out the night. Each flake is another second ticking by, an urgent whisper against the silence between us. They cling to Lexi's hair, turning golden strands into frosted tendrils, and settle on her lashes like delicate crystals. With a mutual sigh, our lips part, and there's this ache, raw and new, as if parting is leaving a piece of myself behind.

"Looks like we're about to get snowed in," I say, my breath fogging the air, a white cloud mingling with hers.

Lexi's arms are still looped around my neck, her body pressed close to mine for warmth, but now there's a shiver that isn't entirely from the cold. "We should probably head back before it gets worse."

There's a reluctance in her voice, one that echoes inside me, raging against the storm that threatens to separate us. I nod, not trusting myself to speak just yet, because pulling away feels a hell of a lot like losing something I've only just found. I wonder suddenly, sharply, if she's kissed Noah—but then, I push the question away. She's here with me now.

"Right," I manage to grunt out, finally. But neither of us moves, caught in the gravity of each other's orbit. It's as if we're suspended in those moments after a game-winning goal when the crowd erupts and everything else fades away—except this is more intense, more personal.

Then the wind picks up, howling past us like a warning shot. The cabin light flickers in the distance, our lone beacon in the encroaching storm.

"Damn weather," she mutters, and I catch the glint of disappointment in her eyes, mirroring my own.

"Mother Nature's got terrible timing," I reply, trying to muster a grin.

I grab Lexi's hand, the snow crunching under our boots as we launch into a clumsy sprint toward the cabin. The world is a blur of white, every flake stinging like tiny darts on my exposed skin. She's laughing, the sound somehow rising above the roar of the wind, and it's infectious, pulling a chuckle from me despite the chill that bites at my bones.

"Watch out for the—" I shout, but it's too late. Her foot catches on something hidden beneath the snow, and we're tumbling, a mess of limbs and breathless laughter. Somehow, in the tumble, we end up sprawled across the ground, her on top of me, my arms instinctively wrapping around her to break her fall. We're both gasping, not just from the shock of the fall, but from the absurdity of it all.

"Graceful," she teases, her breath coming out in visible puffs that mingle with mine.

"Years of training," I manage to say, though the cold is starting to leach into my senses, numbing fingertips that are still laced with hers.

"Your shoulder…"

"I'm fine," I assure.

We scramble to our feet, brushing off the snow that clings to us like a second skin. The wind is relentless, howling around us as if angered by our intrusion into its domain. It's a beast of a storm, the kind that could easily swallow two foolish hearts whole.

"Come on!" I urge, tugging her forward. We half walk, half skate across the icy terrain. And even as the cold seeps deeper, threatening to freeze the moment in time, I can't help but feel the warmth of possibility between us—a heat that no winter can truly touch.

The door slams shut behind us, cutting off the howl of the wind like a switch flipped to silence. My chest heaves, my breaths coming out in white clouds that quickly dissipate in the warmth of the cabin. Lexi's beside me, her body radiating heat despite the icicles practically forming in her sandy blonde hair.

"Safe," she gasps with the thrill of our mad dash through the storm. She's all flushed cheeks and adrenaline, looking more alive than anyone has a right to after facing nature's fury.

"Never doubted it for a second," I lie, trying to steady my own breathing. The truth is, for a moment out there, I wasn't sure if we'd make it back without becoming human snowmen. But Lexi's laugh, free and unguarded, makes every numb finger and frozen toe worth it.

"Your poker face needs work, Jacobs," she teases, brushing snowflakes from her lashes. Even now, she challenges me, but there's an ease between us that wasn't there before—the storm outside somehow melting walls inside. And the kiss didn't hurt, either.

"Maybe," I concede, "or maybe I just play a different game when it comes to you."

Her smile falters, replaced by something deeper, more intense. There's a question in her gaze, one I'm not sure I have the answer to yet. It's crazy how fast things change—how quickly a person can become your storm and shelter all at once.

"Let's join the others," she suggests, breaking the spell between us. "Before they start sending out a search party."

"Right." I nod, though part of me wants to pull her back into the storm, away from prying eyes and expectations.

As we step into the crowded living room, I catch a look—a silent exchange between Lexi and Noah that sends a sharp pang through me. It's nothing, just a flicker, but suddenly I'm all too aware of the thin ice we're skating on. He definitely has eyes for her, and that could get…complicated.

Great, I think as I watch her disappear into the crowd, *just great*.

I grab a beer from the cooler, the cold of the can seeping into my hand. I take a long drink, letting the bitterness wash over me, wondering how the hell I'm going to navigate the treacherous path ahead. Because falling for Lexi isn't part of the plan, but neither is watching her dance out of reach.

And the storm outside? It's got nothing on the one brewing in my chest.

CHAPTER EIGHT: LEXI

I'm still tasting the ghost of Wes's kiss, a mix of mint and rebellion, when we're all back in the arena Monday morning. The ice rink echoes with the early-morning sounds of hockey practice—pucks slamming against the boards, skates carving into the frosty surface. I had been floating on a cloud of dangerous attraction all weekend, but now, being back here feels like walking into an emotional minefield.

The memory of his lips pressing against mine sends a jolt through me that's half thrill, half dread. It was impulsive, intense, and everything I expected from Wes Jacobs, the guy who plays by his own rules. And yet, the slow dance and the warm expression on Noah's face keeps flashing in my mind, his kind-hearted captain's gaze as genuine as his sportsmanship on the ice.

"Hey, Turner! Focus!" A voice shouts from across the rink, snapping me out of my reverie.

As I stand up to look for the source of the lilting words, the cold air bites at my cheeks. But it's nothing compared to the chill that settles over me when I see Cassidy Harper gliding onto the ice. She's like a winter storm personified—beautiful, dangerous, and entirely unpredictable. Her every move screams privilege, from her perfectly styled hair that never seems to fall out of place, even under a beanie, to the designer coat she shrugs off and hands to some adoring minion. What is she doing at practice? She should be at her own practice. Cheerleaders never attend the rough-and-tumble morning drills.

I know Cassidy from high school. She and her "squad" were the popular girls in school, the cliched crew that only dated jocks and spent their time primping in the bathroom between classes and bullying anyone who didn't fit their criteria—which was ever-changing and mostly based on looks and how much your parents made. I never measured up, not that I cared. But I've always found Cassidy nearly intolerable.

And then she does something totally unexpected—she makes a beeline for Noah. My stomach drops as I watch her reach him, her hand brushing his arm in a way that's just shy of possessive. Her laughter rings out clear and melodic, but to me, it sounds like a siren's call—one that spells disaster.

"Turner, you okay?" someone asks, but I can't tear my eyes away from the scene unfolding before me. Noah looks caught off guard, his smile polite but strained as Cassidy leans in, whispering something that prompts a furrowed brow from him.

Jealousy is a spiked ball in my chest, each breath pushing the points deeper. I want to look away, to skate off this sudden, sharp pain, but I can't. I'm frozen, watching the girl who's had everything handed to her on a silver platter make her move on the one guy who's shown me kindness without expecting anything in return.

"Lexi?" The voice is closer now, tinged with concern. I finally manage to break the spell, glancing over to see one of the assistant coaches peering at me with a frown. "You sure you're good to go?"

"Yeah," I say, pushing past the hurt that threatens to spill over. "Just thought I saw something." But it's more than something. It's a clear picture of where I stand—or where I don't.

"Can you help Hartley suit up?" the assistant asks, and I nod woodenly.

I tighten the straps on Dean Hartley's gear, my fingers working mechanically, weaving through laces and buckles. He grunts—a sort of thanks, I guess—and I nod, keeping my face neutral. Inside, I'm a mess of tangled strings, each one pulling in a different direction and threatening to unravel me completely.

"Good job, Turner," Dean smirks, giving me an exaggerated pat on the back. "Got your head in the game?"

"Always," I retort, but it's a lie. My head is anywhere but here. It's stuck between the lingering burn of Wes's lips and the sting of seeing Cassidy Harper cozying up to Noah. I feel like an outsider in my own life, unsure where the boundaries lie, or if there are any left at all.

"Hey Lexi," Wes calls out from across the rink, and I brace myself. His voice is a siren—it's come to signify both danger and desire, and I never know which I'm sailing toward. I glance up to catch him watching me, that half-smirk playing on his lips, as if he knows exactly what kind of chaos he's stirred within me.

"Need me for something?" I ask, my tone clipped. Professional distance is my armor now, even though I want nothing more than to peel away the layers of doubt and insecurity that have settled over me like frost.

"Thought you might check my tape job," he says, patting his shoulder. It's an excuse, we both know it, but I walk over anyway because when Wes Jacobs asks, I somehow find it impossible to say no. I grab a roll of kinesiology tape.

My hands take over, pulling the collar of his jersey aside, adjusting the tape here and there. It's a dance I know by heart—distraction through action. Each strip I smooth down is another thought I push aside: thoughts of Wes, thoughts of Noah, thoughts of what it means to be caught between two very different worlds.

"Looks good," I finally say, stepping back. The moment feels heavy, charged with unspoken words and what-ifs. But I can't afford to dwell on them, not when there's work to be done.

"Thanks," Wes replies, and I can tell he's trying to read me, to find an opening in the walls I've built up overnight. But I'm determined to keep them standing, at least until I figure out how to navigate the minefield that is my personal life without blowing everything up—including my future career.

"Let's keep it professional, okay?" I add, and Wes nods, a shadow crossing his features. He gets it, I think. He has to.

"Of course, Turner," he says, and there's an edge to his voice that lets me know he's not just talking about the tape job.

As practice progresses, I throw myself into the work, tending to pulled muscles and bruised egos with equal fervor. Each ice pack I apply, every encouraging word I offer—it's all part of the role I play here. After practice, I turn from the main rink, my cheeks flushed with cold and exertion. I stomp my feet to shake off the numbness, stealing another glance at Noah and Cassidy as I head to the back hallway. They're deep in conversation now, her hand resting lightly on his chest. He laughs at something she says, but the sound doesn't quite reach his eyes.

Noah looks up and catches me watching.

"Lex, wait up!" Noah calls after me, his voice tinged with an urgency that knots my insides. He reaches up and pulls Cassidy's hand away.

"Can't, busy day!" I call back, not trusting myself to handle a close-up encounter. I need space, distance – anything to avoid watching the guy I might have feelings for cozy up to someone else.

As I weave through the corridors, I remind myself that this is how it has to be. I can't control their actions, only my reactions. Lexi Turner, intern extraordinaire, the girl who has her act together even when her heart's a jumbled mess. And maybe, just maybe, if I focus hard enough on being that person, I'll start to feel like her too.

CHAPTER NINE: LEXI

I stumble into the dorm room, my muscles screaming from the weekend retreat's relentless activities and the strain of having to get up and back on schedule early this morning for regular practice. Then, after practice, a full slate of classes. I'm wiped out, but there's a buzz under my skin, an electric current of confusion.

"Lexi!" The voice snaps me out of my thoughts. There, perched on her bed like some kind of gossip hawk, is Jenna, my roommate. Her eyes are wide, too bright, like she's sitting on a jackpot at a Vegas slot machine.

"Guess what?" She practically vibrates with the need to spill whatever tea she's holding onto. "You will not believe who's officially an item."

"Give me a sec," I grunt, dropping my duffel bag with a thud that echoes off the cinderblock walls. I peel off my jersey, swapping it for a more breathable tank top, but before I can even breathe out, Jenna's words hit me like a rogue puck.

"Cassidy Harper and Noah Bishop. Public. Official. PDA and all. Did you know this? They were totally sucking face on the quad for all to see. She was like a leech on him."

The exhaustion clinging to my bones morphs into a sucker punch of shock that rattles through me. Cassidy and Noah? My brain fumbles to make sense of it, the way it struggles to calculate a complex play on the ice when you've got a fraction of a second to act.

"Are you kidding me?" It's all I manage, my voice a strange cocktail of disbelief and something else I can't quite place—a sour twist in the pit of my stomach.

"Nope," Jenna chirps, oblivious to the inner chaos she's just unleashed. "Saw them myself, east side of the quad by the library. It's the talk of the campus. No one even knew that they hung out outside of games."

I blink, trying to picture it—Cassidy Harper, with her air of untouchable snobbery, wrapped up in Noah's strong captain's arms.

He's supposed to be the good guy, the leader who plays fair. And Cassidy... she's as far from fair play as you can get.

"Wow," is all I say because what else is there? The news sits heavy, a lead puck in my gut. Noah Bishop, off the market and into the hands of my rival. She says sports medicine is her passion, but I think she's looking to land a pro hockey husband and retire her degree early. Not that it'll leave her with any burdens—her muckety-muck alumni parents are rich enough that there are no student loans to hang over her highlighted head. I shake my head, trying to dislodge the image, the unwelcome emotion it stirs within me.

"Right?" Jenna nods, her eyes gleaming. "I mean, who would have thought?"

Not me, certainly not me.

In fact, jealousy gnaws at me like a hungry rink rat. It's absurd. I shouldn't care who Noah dates—it's none of my business. But as much as I tell myself this, my insides churn with uncertainty. Why does the thought of them together make my blood simmer just below boiling?

"Seriously, they're like, perfect for each other. Hockey royalty meets cheer queen," Jenna adds, laughter bubbling in her tone.

Hockey royalty. The words echo in my head, mocking me. Is that all we are? Titles and status? I've spent so much time around the rink, I can practically breathe hockey stats, but right now, I want nothing more than to escape the suffocating culture of it all.

I grab a jacket to throw on over my tank top and then my backpack. I have to get out—the dorm room is too small and closing in.

"I'm going to study," I say, and I don't wait for Jenna to reply before I'm out the door.

***

I shove open the door to the library, the scent of old books and desperation for high GPAs hitting me instantly. I'm here with one mission: to drown out Cassidy's smug voice that's bound to echo in my head until I can refocus on what matters—my future as a sports medicine expert. Intern hours alone aren't going to get me into a graduate program, nor a good job. I still need the grades.

"Lexi!" The voice I've been dreading slices through the hushed whispers of diligent students. Cassidy Harper leans against a bookshelf like she owns the place, her hazel eyes glinting with something akin to victory. "Fancy seeing you here."

"Libraries are for studying," I quip, not missing a beat. "You should try it sometime."

Her laugh tinkles through the silence, drawing annoyed glances. "Oh, Lexi, always so witty. But I'm here for a much more exciting reason. Have you heard the news?"

"Unless it's about groundbreaking treatments for ACL injuries, I'm not interested," I reply, but my heart thuds treacherously against my ribs.

"Oh, yes. Always the little class go-getter. But this is even better. Noah asked me out," she beams, flipping her hair over her shoulder. There's a deliberate pause as she gauges my reaction. "Officially."

"Congrats," I force out, the word feeling like a slapshot to the gut. "He's a great guy."

"Isn't he just?" Cassidy drawls, eyes narrowing slightly as if she's trying to read my playbook. "I heard you and he were getting real close this past weekend. I was hoping you weren't heartbroken, since we're the talk of the campus."

"Power couple goals," I say mechanically, my sarcasm skating on thin ice. She doesn't need to know how much her words sting, that they're like a puck ricocheting in my chest. "And Noah and I are just friends."

"Oh." Her lips mou. "Anyway, I'll let you get back to... whatever it is you do. We wouldn't want your grades dropping because of little old me. That hurts your scholarship money, right?" Cassidy says sweetly, though the barb is there, hidden under layers of faux concern.

"My grades are fine," I retort, turning away before she can see the cracks in my façade. I don't give her the satisfaction of looking back as I march toward the back of the library, where the study carrels promise solitude and, hopefully, distraction.

Finding an empty carrel, I drop into the chair with less grace than usual. I pull out my biomechanics textbook, the pages filled with diagrams of joints and ligaments, a world where things make sense, where there's a clear cause and effect. If only human relationships were as straightforward as a knee joint.

I dive into the material, letting terms like 'tibia' and 'femur' replace 'Cassidy' and 'Noah' in my mind. My notes become more frenzied, my handwriting sloppier as I scribble down information on muscle fiber types and injury prevention. Each word is a balm, each sentence a strategy to keep the game in play.

Hours pass, maybe minutes—it's hard to tell when you're lost in a world of anatomical structures and potential treatment plans. But one thing is clear: this is where I belong, among these textbooks and the quiet hum of knowledge-seeking souls. This is the rink where I skate circles around life's messy checks into the boards.

And when I finally close my textbook, the initial sting of Cassidy's words has dulled. I'm sore from the hit, sure, but not down. Not out. I'm still in this game, and I plan to come out a winner.

My phone buzzes from its forgotten spot under a pile of notecards, jolting me back to reality. I swipe away the remnants of physiology diagrams from my vision, squinting at the bright screen. It's a message from Jenna, with her typical flurry of emojis that somehow always seem to capture the urgency of college gossip.

Forgot to ask you about Wes!

What about him? I text back, mind still echoing with the remnants of biomechanics and ligaments, not ready for another round of campus drama.

His mom's sick. Like, really sick. I heard it from his RA.

The textbooks on my lap suddenly feel heavier, dense with concern rather than knowledge. *How sick are we talking?*

Pretty bad, from what I've heard.

Thanks for letting me know, I murmur, my thoughts already on Wes, on that brooding intensity he tries so hard to guard, the shadow behind those ice-blue eyes, a hint of something deeper than his usual rebellious charm.

I stand up, packing up my fortress of study materials. My fingers hover over my phone, a battle between wanting to give him space and the pull of compassion that tugs at my chest. Wes is strong, sure, but everyone has their breaking point.

Hope he'll be okay, Jenna says.

Me too. And without overthinking it, I tap out a quick message to Wes.

Hey Wes, just heard about your mom. I'm really sorry. If you need someone to talk to or anything, I'm here.

It's simple, nothing fancy—just an offer of support, a lifeline thrown across the chasm of pride and pretense. I hit send before I can second-guess myself. Wes might not take it, might not even want it, but it's out there now, hanging in the digital ether between us.

Settling back into my chair, I pick up a pen, but my focus has shifted. Now, my heart is racing, wondering if it's him, if he'll let down that guard just a fraction and let me in. The phone buzzes against my desk, and I lunge for it like a goalie diving for a rogue puck. It's Wes.

Can we talk? His text is uncharacteristically vulnerable, stripped of the bravado he so often wears like armor.

Of course, I reply. *Coffee shop on the east side of the quad?*

Give me 10.

I'm already tying my sneakers before the message fully registers. My heart hammers with a cocktail of nerves and adrenaline—not unlike the pre-game jitters before hitting the ice. This isn't about hockey, though; this is real life, with stakes that feel immeasurably higher.

The crisp evening air bites at my cheeks as I walk briskly to the agreed spot. The coffee shop is quiet, the usual chatter from inside subdued. Wes stands by an outside bench, his posture tense, like he's bracing himself against more than just the winter chill.

"Hey," I breathe out, approaching him with cautious steps.

"Lexi." He acknowledges me with a nod and a strained half-smile. "Thanks for coming."

"Of course." I sit beside him, giving him the space to start when he's ready.

He takes a deep breath, and it's like watching the dam break, words flowing freely. "My mom... she's been diagnosed with cancer. It's bad, Lexi. Really bad."

The raw pain in his usually guarded gaze slices through me. "Wes, I—I'm so sorry."

He shrugs a feeble attempt to deflect the sympathy. "We've always just had each other, you know? I don't have a clue how to deal with this."

"Nobody knows how to handle something like that," I say softly, reaching out to tentatively place a hand over his. "But you're not alone, okay? You've got your team, friends... me."

"Me," he echoes, turning his hand to clasp mine, and there's a shift in the air between us. For a moment, it's as though the rest of the world fades away, leaving only the two of us locked in an understanding too profound for words.

After a beat, he continues, his voice steadier but still tinged with fear. "She wants to fight it, go through all the treatments, but... what if it's not enough?"

"Then you'll know you did everything you could. And she will, too. That's all anyone can do, Wes."

He nods, the tension easing from his shoulders ever so slightly. "Yeah. Yeah, you're right." He stands, his hand still in mine. “I gotta go. My next class is in ten. I’ll see you at the game tonight.”

And then, he's gone, our encounter brief but meaning…what? It's only when he releases my hand that I realize how much I wanted to hold onto it. How much I wanted to be that source of strength for him.

CHAPTER TEN: LEXI

Game night, and the roar of the crowd swallows my thoughts as I look around the arena, a sea of cheering fans undulating like a living thing. The air buzzes with electricity, thick with anticipation. The bright lights glint off the ice, a stark white stage set for tonight's battle. Players zip across the rink, their sharpened blades carving arcs of frost, their bodies colliding with the force of storms clashing.

We're tied up, and I couldn't be tenser.

"Go Thunderbirds!" hollers the opposing section of blue and gold, the chant rippling through the stands like a wave. On the bench, my guys slam their sticks against the boards, a rallying cry the Ashville Aces on the ice. I'm on my feet, leaning over the boards, every muscle tensed, every sense honed in on the play. The puck drops, and it's like releasing a spring wound tight—chaos erupts. Sticks clash, players weave an intricate dance of raw power and finesse. The game is a language I speak fluently, each pass and shot a word, each save a punctuation mark in this story of sweat and steel.

"Come on, come on..." I whisper, tracking our lead scorer as he darts toward the goal. I can't help but get caught up in the thrill, the chase of victory that runs parallel to my own mission. But beneath the excitement, there's always that undercurrent of readiness, the professional vigilance waiting to spring into action.

Puck on a stick, Noah glides across the ice like a force of nature, sidestepping a defender with the ease of a seasoned captain. Cassidy screams his name girlishly from the side of the rink. I can feel my eyes roll. Noah pivots, aiming for that shot that might just be the game-changer, it happens—a collision, brutal and unplanned. His figure skews awkwardly, colliding with an opposing player whose bulk sends shockwaves through the rink. I wince from my vantage point; I can almost feel the twist of his ankle from here, the way his body contorts unnaturally before he crashes to the ice.

"Damn it," I mutter under my breath, already anticipating the sharp sting of pain he must be feeling. I see him grimace, hand reaching down to cradle the joint in a silent confirmation of injury. The arena's collective gasp is a background hum to the pounding in my ears—this is what I've been bracing for.

But there's no time to dwell because, in the next heartbeat, Wes, looking back at Noah, takes a hard check into the boards that would have lesser men seeing stars. The Thunderbird who checked him spins away, sneering, and Wes staggers forward, hand clasping his shoulder, a grimace etched deep into his features.

"Trainee!" The call from Drew snaps me into motion. "Bishop first. I'll take Jacobs."

I'm over the barrier and onto the ice before my brain fully processes the move. My skates bite into the frozen surface, propelling me forward with urgency.

Stay calm, Lexi. They need you focused, I remind myself, even as my heart races and adrenaline surges through my veins.

I reach Noah, dropping to my knees beside him. "Talk to me, Captain," I say, trying to keep my voice steady as I assess the damage. He tries to mask the pain with a tight smile, but his eyes betray him.

"Twisted it again—same one—when I landed," he grunts, and I nod, hands already at work.

"Okay, let's get this stabilized." I'm all business, the world narrowing to the task at hand. I secure his ankle with practiced efficiency, the cold pack in my kit providing temporary relief. As I wrap the compress around the swelling joint, I can feel the stare of a few thousand spectators boring into me, but they fade away—it's just Noah, his ankle, and the ice beneath us.

"Keep pressure on this," I instruct, locking eyes with him to ensure the message gets through. He nods, gritting his teeth against the discomfort, but trust shines through the pain. It's a look I've earned, one that speaks louder than any cheer from the crowd.

Beside us, at rink's edge, Cassidy is calling Noah's name, sounding hysterical. I don't have time for her. A sharp whistle pierces the charged air, and I'm up again—this time to Wes, at Drew's side. Wes's brooding expression is twisted in pain as he clutches his shoulder, and my gut clenches. I glide over, skates carving a path on the ice, my medical bag bumping against my side.

"Hey there, tough guy," I quip, trying to ease the tension as I kneel beside him. "How's the arm feeling?"

"Like Dean's been using it for punching practice," Wes grumbles, but his attempt at humor doesn't quite reach his eyes.

"Can you move it at all?"

"Bit stiff," he hisses as Drew palpates the area, watching his face for signs of increased pain. It's not dislocated—that much is clear—but a hard check like that could mean a sprain or even a tear.

"We need to reduce the swelling first, figure out the rest later," Drew says.

"All right, we're going to ice this now," I inform Wes, reaching for a cold compress from my kit. "You know the drill—cold now, heat later."

"Always so commanding," he teases weakly, but complies, allowing me to position the cold pack against his shoulder. I secure it with a wrap, ensuring it won't slip while he's benched.

"Try not to flex or rotate it too much," Drew advise, and my gaze locks onto Wes's, which seems to flicker with a mix of pain and stubborn resolve. "I'll check on you after the period ends."

"Thanks, Doc," Wes says, the corner of his mouth lifting ever so slightly. Then, he looks at me as I add another strip of tape. "Guess you're not just a pretty face, after all."

"Keep your charm, Jacobs. Save it for when you're not in agony," I shoot back, though a smirk tugs at my lips. I cast a quick glance back at Noah, who's now on the bench, watching us with an unreadable expression.

"Can you get yourself to the box?" I say, already thinking two steps ahead.

He nods, pushing up with his good side.

As we skate back to the bench, my mind races while the match roars on around us. The blur of the game swoops around me, a symphony of shouts and the slice of skates against ice that vibrates right through my bones. I point at the bench beside Noah and address Wes.

"Sit. Down." My tone brooks no argument, and surprisingly, he complies, flashing me a half-grin that doesn't quite reach those piercing blue eyes.

"Never thought I'd be so glad to see you skating toward me," Wes admits, his voice a low rumble. "You're like some kind of... hockey angel."

"Only you could turn an injury into a pick-up line, Jacobs," I quip, but I'm checking his pupils, making sure he's not just putting on a brave face. "Stay put. Like Drew said, we need to reassess after this period, okay?"

"Can't make any promises, Turner," he replies, but there's a note of respect there that wasn't before. Even Wes Jacobs can acknowledge a job well done.

I leave him with a stern look, already turning back to Noah. Two of our best on the sidelines and the game's intensity hasn't dropped one iota. I keep one eye on the clock, counting down the minutes until I can properly assess their injuries off-ice.

"Alexis Turner, folks," the announcer's voice booms suddenly during a brief lull, echoing around the arena. "Showing once again why she's an indispensable part of the Aces family!"

A cheer erupts from the crowd, a wave of noise that crashes over me, but I don't let it distract. Flattery won't help these guys heal faster.

I rewrap Noah's ankle, double-checking the support, then catch Wes trying to test his shoulder's mobility out of the corner of my eye.

"Jacobs!" I snap, sharper than intended, and he winces, settling back against the boards. "If you mess up my handiwork..."

"You'll what? Bench me?" he challenges, but there's no heat in it. He knows I'm right.

"Try me," I say with a smirk, and for a moment, we're not athlete and therapist, but two rivals who understand each other better than anyone might guess.

As the buzzer sounds, signaling the end of the period, I'm already planning. Noah needs an X-ray, and Wes might be looking at an MRI if that shoulder doesn't improve. But for now, they're both stable, and that's a small victory.

"I'm going back in," Wes announces abruptly, right as Coach Thompson glides over, a hard look etched on his face.

"No," I interject, my voice steady with conviction. "You're both out for the rest of this period."

Coach Thompson studies me intently, then shifts his gaze to Noah and Wes. "We need you two back out there," he insists in his gruff voice.

Against my better judgement, I feel a surge of frustration. "You need them healthy more," I counter. "A few minutes on the bench now might mean they can play the next game."

Despite my passionate objection, Coach Thompson seems unmoved. He's a seasoned warrior of the ice, hardened by decades of hollering from the sidelines and echoing locker-room pep talks. "This game is crucial, Alexis," he growls, his beady eyes darting between us.

"I am fully aware, Coach," I retort, crossing my arms over my chest. "But pushing them now isn't going to do any good."

"You're here to keep them in the game, not bench them," he says pointedly before turning to the injured men beside me. "Are you two all right?"

Noah grimaces, nodding as he tests his ankle. I glare at him. He should know better. Wes just shoots me a challenging look, back straight, jaw set. He's ready to throw himself back in the fray, regardless of the consequences.

"I'm good," Noah mutters, but his pained grimace tells me otherwise. No one seems to read him as well as I can.

"Good enough for me," Coach Thompson declares, giving them both an approving nod. He skates off towards the bench, leaving me simmering with frustration and worry.

"Wes… Noah…" I begin, my voice cracking slightly under the weight of my concern. "Please let me do my job."

"You do yours, Turner," Wes interrupts, his icy gaze locking with mine. "We'll handle ours." His smile is sharp, full of reckless defiance.

"I'm not sitting out the third," Noah chimes in, his tone not as harsh as Wes's but firm nonetheless. His easy smile belies the pain I know he's in.

Then, they're both up and out, and the crowd cheers, drowning out any new objections. The puck zips across the ice like it's got a life of its own, and Wes chases it down with the ferocity of a man who hasn't just had his shoulder popped back into place minutes before. I can't help but wince when he takes a hit, body slamming against the boards, but he doesn't falter. If anything, the contact seems to ignite something within him, and he's back in possession, maneuvering around the opposition with an agility that belies any pain he might be feeling.

"Unbelievable," I breathe, pride and frustration swelling in my chest for this relentless star forward who refuses to be benched by injury or by *me*. I know I'm just an intern, but the disrespect stings.

On the other side of the rink, Noah orchestrates the team with the precision of a maestro, ankle taped up tight and brace concealed beneath layers of padding. When he snipes a shot from the blue line, threading the needle through a sea of sticks and skates, the puck finds the back of the net, and the arena erupts into a cacophony of cheers. He raises his stick in triumph, and though his eyes are hidden beneath his helmet, I know there's a glint of satisfaction there.

"Nice shot!" I can't stop myself from shouting, even though he can't hear me over the din.

As the match surges forward, every check and dodge, every sharp turn and slapshot, I'm right there with them. My gaze never lingers too long on one; I'm constantly scanning, ready to leap into action should either show signs of worsening.

When the final buzzer sounds, signaling the end of the game, the score in our favor, the rush of relief is almost dizzying. Noah and Wes make their way back to the bench, their strides less sure now, the adrenaline ebbing away to reveal the true extent of their injuries.

Coach Thompson intercepts us before Drew and I can rush over to my wounded warriors. "You've done enough, Turner," he warns, his voice stern and authoritative. His brows knit tightly, a clear sign that he's not in the mood for argument. He nods at Drew. "Leave 'em be. Meet me in my office. Now."

Drew's jaw tenses, but he nods, curtly, and he's gone in a flash. I can only hope he'll go to bat for the right course of action. I think he will.

But that leaves me and Thompson alone. A sudden chill washes over me despite the heat of the stadium lights. "I was just doing my job," I defend hastily.

His gaze narrows further, casting a long shadow on his weathered face. "You're here to assist, not to interfere with my players."

My heart skips a beat at his words. The implication isn't lost on me. I'm just an intern. My instinct is to counter his remark, to defend my actions, but the icy coolness of his stare silences me.

"I won't hesitate to bench you if you step out of line again," Coach Thompson adds, voice steely. "Do I make myself clear?"

"Crystal," I manage to reply, swallowing around the lump forming in my throat.

The euphoria from the victory is quickly evaporating, replaced by a gnawing worry. Biting my lower lip, I nod at him and step back, watching as he strides off towards the staff offices.

They're both slumped on the bench now, exhaustion seeping from every pore, their faces glistening with sweat. The crowd is still chanting their names, but I doubt either of them can hear it over the thundering pulse in their ears. Noah rubs at his ankle, a grimace twisting his handsome features. Wes's hand is pressed against his shoulder, his lips pressed into a thin line as he attempts to quell the pain rippling through him. It's clear that they've pushed themselves beyond their limits.

But I can't rush over to them. My place is here, on the sidelines, torn between wanting to ensure they're okay and respecting Coach Thompson's warning. Around me, the celebration carries on, oblivious to my inner turmoil. The team's win is celebrated with raucous cheers and laughter, the air thick with excitement and relief. I can't help but feel that it all rings hollow when the cost is so high.

With a heavy heart, I force myself to turn away, to focus on packing up the medical kit, which now looks woefully inadequate for what may lie ahead. The metallic clink of the instruments echoes my loneliness amidst the jubilant crowd.

CHAPTER ELEVEN: WES

I'm sprawled on my bed, the ceiling above me a blank canvas for the shadow-play of my worries. My phone is a cold weight in my hand, its screen dark and silent, reflecting nothing of the storm brewing inside me. Mom's voice still echoes in my ears, her forced cheerfulness not enough to mask the fatigue that clung to each word. It's like she's fading with every call, slipping through my fingers, and I'm miles away, powerless. She doesn't want me to come home—thinking of me, my future, school, hockey.

A vibration jolts me from my thoughts. A text message flashes up. Lexi. *Can we talk?* There's an urgency in those simple words, a silent plea that doesn't go unnoticed despite the fog of my own troubles.

"Sure," I type back, more out of reflex than desire. "Coffee shop again?" My thumb hovers over the send button, reluctant. Talking means opening up, letting someone see the cracks. But it's Lexi. If anyone gets the chaos of this life, it's her. The girl who rebounded from a shattered knee to chase a new dream, who knows what it's like when life body checks you into the boards.

Sent.

I push off the bed, wincing, a sudden urge to move overtaking the inertia and the pain of my shoulder. The MRI showed nothing permanent—but Drew says I was damned lucky, the way I pushed it. I'm not sure how Jacobs made out, but I do know that he had to be in more pain than me, with that annoying Cassidy hanging all over him in the med office.

This room feels too small for my restlessness, too full of the silence that echoes with the unsaid. I need to get out, need the sharp bite of winter to clear my head. Maybe talking to someone will help me find some perspective. Mom wouldn't want me wallowing anyway. She's all about facing challenges head-on, with a mixture of stubbornness and grace I can never seem to replicate. But maybe, just maybe, with Lexi, I can try.

I shove my hands into the pockets of my jacket, head bowed against the cold as I make my way through the campus. Each step feels like I'm skating through slush, slow and dragging, the weight of worry for Mom grounding me more than gravity ever could. The night air bites at any exposed skin, and with each breath, I can almost feel the chill settling in my bones.

The snow underfoot offers a soft crunch, a constant reminder that life goes on, indifferent to the turmoil churning inside me. Students laugh and chatter around me, their voices muffled by the knit caps and scarves wrapped tight against the winter wind. They're in their own worlds, oblivious to the storm in mine.

"Hey, Wes," Lexi's voice cuts through the frosty air as I approach our spot. She's already there, leaning against the thick trunk of the oak tree out front, arms crossed. Even in the dim light, I can see the concern etched across her face.

"Lexi," I nod, stuffing my hands deeper into my coat pockets. "You wanted to talk?"

She unfolds her arms and steps closer, green eyes searching mine. "I've noticed you've been off lately. More than usual, I mean." A wry smile tugs at the corner of her mouth, but it's a fake. "Is everything okay?"

"Define 'okay,'" I say, deflecting with sarcasm—my go-to defense mechanism.

"Come on, Wes. Don't do that." Her tone is soft, but firm. "That stunt today, taking that risk—I know something's up. Is it about your mom?"

I hesitate, feeling the wall I've built around myself starting to crumble. There's no point in pretending with Lexi; she sees right through me. "It's just... things aren't great," I admit, my voice barely above a whisper. It's the most I've said to anyone about it, and even this feels like revealing too much.

"Talk to me," she urges gently, stepping even closer. "You don't have to go through this alone."

There's a battle raging within me: the desire to keep everything locked down tight versus the need to let someone in. But it's Lexi—steadfast, unflappable Lexi—who's asking. And damn it if part of me doesn't want to spill everything to her, to let her shoulder some of this burden.

"Her treatments aren't working the way they hoped," I choke out, the words tasting bitter on my tongue. "We're running out of options, and... I don't know what to do. She doesn't want me there, though. I grew up poor, Lex. Without my scholarship money, no college. And without hockey, no scholarship. So that *risk*..."

"Hey..." Lexi's hand finds mine, her grip warm and reassuring. "You're doing everything you can. Your mom knows that. And I'm here for you, Wes. Whatever you need."

I never thought I'd find relief in sharing my fears, especially not with someone who could bench-press them away with such ease. But as Lexi stands with me, her presence a beacon in the shadow of my worries, I can't help but think that maybe, just maybe, I'm not as alone as I thought.

I slump down onto the frost-covered bench, drawing in a breath that feels like inhaling icicles. Lexi sits beside me, her body radiating a warmth that seems to defy the winter chill encasing us. I glance at her, and there's this earnest concern in her eyes that makes my chest tighten.

"Mom's always been the strong one," I say, my voice trembling despite my efforts to steady it. "Now she's so frail, hooked up to machines, and I can't do anything." My throat constricts as if the cold has crept inside, turning words into fragile things that might shatter if spoken too loudly.

"Her laughter used to fill our whole apartment," I continue, the memories spilling out of me now like water from a dam that's finally burst. "She'd dance around the kitchen, terrible moves and all, just to make me laugh."

Lexi's hand finds its way over mine, enveloping it with a comfort that's both foreign and familiar. She doesn't speak—doesn't have to. Her touch says everything her words don't.

"Sometimes I imagine getting the call," I confess, the icy dread that's haunted me for months leaking into my voice. "The one saying she's gone, and I..." My breath hitches, and I can't go on.

We sit in a silence that stretches between us—the kind that's thick with unspoken understanding and shared heartache. The snowfall seems to quiet the world around us, muffling everything until there's nothing left but the two of us and the weight of my reality.

And then, slowly, I feel something shift inside me, like a burden being partitioned, made lighter by the simple act of sharing it. It's not a fix, not a solution, but for the first time in longer than I can remember, the crushing pressure in my chest eases just enough for me to breathe.

"Let's skip the coffee and walk," she suggests.

I nod.

I follow Lexi through the throng of students, away from the solemnity of our earlier conversation. She leads me into the heart of the campus, where the air is laced with laughter and chatter, the kind that seems to come easy to everyone but me. It's like stepping into another world, one painted in vibrant colors against the stark white backdrop of winter.

The quad is adorned with strings of twinkling lights that hang from tree to tree like stars plucked from the night sky. Soft music plays somewhere in the distance, a melody gentle enough not to disrupt the serene scene. I can see my breath in the air, mingling with the scents of pine and hot cocoa—simple pleasures that feel a million miles away from the cold grip of reality.

"Look up," she murmurs suddenly, nodding toward the sky.

Above us, tacked to an archway, hangs a sprig of mistletoe, its green leaves stark against the wooden frame. My heart hitches, and the noise around us fades into a low buzz. There's no escaping the tradition it stands for—a kiss.

"Guess it's meant to be," she teases, her voice lower than before, but I catch the flicker of hesitation.

"Or it's a trap set by the universe." A half-smile tugs at my lips, but my pulse races, betraying my attempt at humor. She's close, too close, and under any other circumstances, I wouldn't hesitate. But there's too much between us now, too many unspoken truths that linger in the space of our silence.

"Maybe," Lexi concedes, her gaze locked on mine. "But aren't you curious?"

"About what?" I ask, though I'm painfully aware of the tension that crackles between us, electric and inviting.

"About whether the universe knows what it's doing." Her words are a challenge, a spark that threatens to ignite the moment into something neither of us may be ready for.

"Are you?" The question slips out, a whisper of desire mixed with the undeniable fear of crossing a line we've so carefully drawn.

"Terrified," she admits, but there's a brave smile on her lips, a silent acknowledgment of the mutual dare hanging above us.

"Good." I swallow hard, inching closer until the heat of her body seeps into mine. "Because so am I."

For a long beat, we simply stand there, our breath mingling in the frosty air, a testament to the connection that's always simmered below the surface. But the moment lingers, heavy with possibility and the sweet promise of something more. Time stands still, the kind of silence that's loud in its anticipation. I feel Lexi's breath hitch as my resolve crumbles like thin ice beneath a heavy skate. It's the tilt of her head, the softness in her gaze that's both an invitation and a surrender. My own heart pounds, a relentless drumbeat urging me forward.

"Lexi," I breathe out, my voice rough with emotion that's been dammed up for far too long.

"Kiss me, Wes," she whispers back, her words a flickering flame to my kindling spirit.

And then, I'm closing the distance, the few inches between us feeling like miles until they're not. My hand finds the curve of her jaw, gentle yet unyielding, as though it's always belonged there. Her skin is warm against the chill of the night, a contrast that sends shivers down my spine.

Our lips touch, and it's like the first true thaw of spring after a harsh Minnesota winter. Soft and tentative at first, but growing bolder with each heartbeat. There's a hunger there, a yearning that's been hidden behind jokes and snappy comebacks. The world narrows down to the press of her mouth against mine, sweet and intoxicating.

The kiss deepens, and it's as if we're both trying to communicate everything we've ever felt in this single moment. The electric spark that ignites between us is palpable, racing through our veins and setting every nerve alight. We're drawing from a well of emotions that's been filled over time with shared glances, heated debates on the ice, and the quiet understanding of two souls intertwined by fate.

When we finally part, it's with a reluctance that speaks volumes. Our foreheads rest together, and we're breathing each other's air, lost in a sea of raw emotion. I can see the galaxies swirling in Lexi's wide, luminous eyes—a mix of excitement, uncertainty, and hope.

"Wow," she exhales, her voice a tender caress that somehow says more than any grand declaration ever could.

"Yeah," I agree, my thumb brushing a stray lock of her hair behind her ear. "Wow."

In this charged silence, under the watchful gaze of the mistletoe, we stand rooted to the spot, unwilling to break the spell that's enveloped us. It's a precipice we're both hesitant and eager to explore, the beginning of something neither of us can quite name but are desperate to discover.

"Under the mistletoe," Lexi murmurs with a laugh that holds the promise of all the banter and flirtation to come, now colored with the hue of romance blooming in the cold winter air.

"Under the mistletoe," I echo, knowing that whatever happens next, this moment—this perfect, fragile moment—has changed everything.

"Better?" Her voice is gentle, an anchor in the swirling sea of my mind.

"Much," I admit, squeezing her hand, feeling the soft warmth of her skin against mine. The touch is grounding, real—more real than the ice beneath my skates or the weight of a puck on my stick.

We stop walking, and without a word, we turn to face each other. It's as if our bodies are drawn together by a magnetic force we can't resist, even if we wanted to. She slips into my arms, fitting perfectly against me, her head resting just below my chin. I wrap her up, holding her close, and for a moment, there's nothing else. No sick mother, no hockey pressures, no uncertain future. Just Lexi.

"Thank you," I murmur into her hair, inhaling the scent of her shampoo mixed with the crisp winter air. "For listening. For... understanding."

Her voice vibrates against my chest, and I can feel her smile. "That's what friends are for, right? And maybe... maybe more than friends?"

"Definitely more," I say with a certainty that surprises me. "I don't know what comes next, but I know I want you in it."

"Come on, superstar," she teases, tugging at my hand as we start moving again. "Let's get you back before you turn into a bruised popsicle. Even Minnesota girls have their limits."

"Lead the way," I say, content to follow her anywhere.

As we walk back to the dorms, our footsteps leaving twin trails in the snow, I realize that this is where I'm meant to be. Right here, with Lexi Turner, her hand in mine, looking forward to whatever the future holds—together. Our laughter is quiet, a shared secret between only us and the night. It's crazy how one kiss can shift everything, how opening up to someone can make you feel like you're not shouldering the world alone anymore. There's something about Lexi—the way she challenges me, pushes me, cares for me—that makes me believe it's possible to face whatever lies ahead.

But I'm not sure what that is—and I'm honestly scared.

CHAPTER TWELVE: LEXI

The mind is a treacherous place when it's cluttered with the heart's indecisions. Noah's warm, reassuring smile flickers in my thoughts, battling against Wes's smoldering, mischievous gaze. Both stir something in me, churn the waters of my usually calm emotional sea. It shouldn't be this complicated, should it? But here I am, caught in the middle of my own romantic power play, and I can't seem to find the right strategy to score the winning goal for my heart.

I was so caught up in Wes's vulnerability, in our kiss—had I said too much?

I step outside the morning after that kiss, the campus nearly deserted during winter break, enveloped in a quiet hush that seems to echo my internal solitude. Snowflakes dance lazily from the sky, a delicate waltz that blankets the world in soft white. The familiar crunch beneath my boots is the only sound, a rhythmic beat punctuating the stillness of the leafless trees standing like silent sentinels guarding the grounds.

I'm due at my Dad's house for Christmas. I'm glad—all this alone time is making me overthink things. The chill nips at my cheeks, turning them rosy—a stark contrast to the tangled web of warmth and confusion brewing inside me. I wrap my arms tighter around myself, as if the pressure could squeeze out the answer like juice from an overripe fruit.

Why does love feel like a game where no one fully understands the rules?

Finding my way to the university's central courtyard, I spot the familiar bench by the frozen fountain, its edges lined with icicles, nature's own holiday decorations. My breath forms tiny clouds in the air as I sit down, my jeans instantly soaking up the cold. But I barely notice; there's warmth in the solace of being alone with my thoughts, even if those thoughts are skating circles around me.

Noah would probably say something poetic about the beauty of winter, while Wes would challenge me to a snowball fight with no boundaries or rules, just the thrill of the moment. Both images bring a smile to my lips, the kind that doesn't quite reach my eyes.

"Get it together, Turner," I murmur, brushing away a rogue snowflake from my eyelash. A determination simmers within me, slow and steady. I'm inching closer to the decision that's been eluding me, the one that feels like it could change the trajectory of my life.

I'm not just choosing between two guys. I'm choosing the path I want my heart to skate on, and hoping against hope, I don't fall through the ice.

I lace my fingers together, pressing the palms down hard against the frigid metal of the bench, as if I can squeeze out the indecision that's taken root deep within me. The icy air bites at my cheeks, a stark contrast to the warmth radiating from the tangled thoughts about Noah and Wes swirling in my head.

Noah's the guy who remembers everyone's birthday, who stops to help a stranger change a tire, even if he's running late. His blue eyes don't just sparkle; they hold promises of safety and shared laughter over cups of steaming hot cocoa. With him, love seems like a partnership, steady and sure.

But then there's Wes, an enigma wrapped in a snowstorm. He's the rush of adrenaline when you're barreling down the ice, the puck at your stick, the goal in sight. His intensity, that smoldering look — it's magnetic, pulling me into a dance that's both dangerous and alluring. Loyalty to his team, his friends, it's etched into every fiber of his being, but he doesn't make promises lightly. Life with Wes would be a whirlwind, unpredictable and fiercely passionate.

I stand up abruptly, my movements jagged, mirroring the chaos inside me. Pacing back and forth, I leave footprints in the freshly fallen snow, each step a silent argument between heart and mind. The pros and cons list forms in my head, as methodical as a well-planned training regimen. Noah's reliability, Wes' fiery independence. Noah's gentle support, Wes' challenging push.

Noah is with someone—even if it doesn't seem something that will go the distance—and Wes isn't.

"Ugh," I groan out loud, my voice breaking the silence around me. There's no clear answer, no flashing sign pointing me where to go. It's like trying to predict where the puck will land on a chaotic face-off — impossible. My heart feels like it's caught in a never-ending overtime, fatigued yet unwilling to concede.

I stop pacing and close my eyes, taking in a deep breath that does little to ease the tightness in my chest. It's a tug-of-war of emotions, each man embodying qualities that I admire, that I long for. How do you choose when part of you will be left on the ice, regardless?

I need to make a choice. But right now, my heart is still undecided, skating on thin ice between two futures, and I'm the only one who can pull it to safety. I stand abruptly, restless energy coursing through me. I pace before the bench, the ghost of each moment with Noah and Wes shadowing me.

"Focus, Lexi," I command myself, feeling the tickle of frustration. "What do you want?"

And it hits me, swift as a breakaway goal. What I want isn't safety or a constant challenge. It's not about being cared for or pushed to excel. It's about partnership, about finding someone who offers both shelter and freedom.

The realization sweeps through me, clearing the fog of hesitation. I want Wes. I want the exhilarating rush of unpredictability he brings, tempered by the depth of connection we share. With him, every day promises a new adventure, a chance to be my most authentic self.

"Okay," I breathe, feeling the weight lift from my shoulders. A smile tugs at my lips, one that feels like the promise of spring in the depths of winter. There's a sense of rightness that settles deep within me, as if all this time my heart knew the answer, and I've finally caught up.

Wes is the risk I'm willing to take, the chapter I'm ready to write. Sure, there will be challenges, but what's love without a little bit of ice to keep things interesting? The possibility of it sends a shiver down my spine that has nothing to do with the chilly weather. I picture us on a road trip to nowhere, the windows down despite the cold, music blaring as we sing off-key to classic rock anthems. We'd laugh at our own terrible voices, the sound lost to the wind and the rush of freedom.

I see us trying every hole-in-the-wall diner and quirky roadside attraction we come across, collecting memories. Wes would insist on snapping pictures, capturing my laughter in the split second before I realize he's taking a photo. And then there are the quiet times: him teaching me the finer points of hockey strategy, patiently explaining plays until I see the game through his eyes. There's depth to Wes that goes unnoticed by most, hidden beneath layers of bravado and charm. But I've seen it—the way he looks at the ice, not just as a player but as a true student of the sport. With him, I'll deepen my love for the game, understanding it not only from the sidelines but from the very heartbeat of the action.

This isn't just about choosing Wes. It's about choosing the version of myself that I want to be—fearless, passionate, and open to the adventures that lie ahead. And as I stand alone amidst the stillness of winter break, I'm filled with a sense of eager anticipation for the first time in too long.

"Ugh," I groan, letting out a laugh that sounds more like defeat than amusement. Here I am, wondering if I'm about to make the biggest mistake of my life. Choosing Wes means embracing the unpredictable, but what if it's too much? What if I'm not cut out for a life that's one part thrill, nine parts chaos?

I close my eyes, take in a deep, steadying breath, and force myself to remember why I'm even considering giving my heart to Wes Jacobs. It's not just the way he makes me laugh, or how he challenges me to shoot for the top shelf every time. It's not solely because he looks at me like I'm the only person in the rink during a game. It's the fire he ignites inside me, the one that burns away all the shoulds and coulds until I'm left with pure want. He sees the fighter in me, the girl who got back up every time she was checked into the boards as a teen. He doesn't just accept my strength—he admires it.

Yet, even as I mull over this decision, I know it won't be easy. Relationships, like hockey games, face off against obstacles and opposition. But isn't that what makes victory worthwhile? The struggle, the effort, the work to reach a goal, together.

Can Wes and I do that—and does he even want forever?

CHAPTER THIRTEEN: WES

Christmas break is over too soon. My time at home with my mom is too short, and soon, I'm back on campus facing another set of issues.

I never thought I'd be the guy to get butterflies, but here I am, feeling like I've got a whole damn sanctuary of them flapping around in my stomach. It's official. I want Lexi Turner, with her whip-smart mouth and eyes that sparkle like fresh ice on a rink, to be my girlfriend. The realization hits me every time I see her name pop up on my phone, and damn if it doesn't send a jolt straight through me.

"Did you expect to lose?" Lexi taunts as we linger in the arena after tonight's game. The chill from the ice permeates the air, and I can hear the distant clash of sticks and skates from players exiting the rink.

"Please," I scoff, wrapping an arm around her shoulders, "the only thing I lost tonight was my patience with the ref's bad calls." Her laugh rings out, clear and infectious, and I can't help but join in.

We settle into two seats, just rows away from the glass, the perfect vantage point that Lexi used tonight to point out plays and analyze movements with the expertise of someone who was born to be part of this world. She leans in close, reliving the game, and her commentary flows over me, a mix of technical terms and passionate exclamations. I watch her more than the game.

"Did you see that cross-check? Totally illegal. And the ref was blind as a bat," she says, shaking her head with a mixture of exasperation and admiration.

"Remind me never to play against you," I quip. "I'd end up with more penalties than minutes on the ice."

She elbows me gently, her grin all sharp edges and challenge. "You'd love it."

The game ended with our team clinching a victory, and the crowd's elation echoed our own. As we spill out of the stadium with the throng of fans, there's an energy between us, crackling and alive like the static before a storm. We decide to walk back instead of calling a ride, not ready to let go of the night just yet. Our steps sync as we make our way through the park that separates the arena from campus. The campus's glow fades behind us, leaving the stars to cast a dim light on the path ahead. Lexi's hand finds mine, her fingers intertwining with mine, a perfect fit.

"Ever think about playing again?" I ask, nodding toward where kids are playing a late-night pick-up game on the frozen pond nearby.

"Every day," she admits, her voice tinged with a longing that mirrors my own for things we've lost. "But then I remember what I'm working toward. Helping others stay in the game... it's the next best thing."

"Better, even," I say, meaning it. Because if anyone can turn a setback into something amazing, it's Lexi.

"Thanks, Wes." She bumps my shoulder with hers, the good one, thankfully, a silent acknowledgment that we're in this together, whatever 'this' turns out to be.

I can't predict the future, but as I look down at Lexi with her hand in mine and her laughter mixing with the crisp night air, I know one thing for sure—I'm willing to face off against anything life throws at us, as long as she's by my side. My breath forms clouds in the chilly air as we leave the echoes of the game behind, the solitude of the park wrapping around us like a blanket. Lexi's laughter from our shared jokes still lingers, an infectious melody that makes my chest feel lighter than it has in years.

"Hey," I start, halting mid-stride. I've never been one for heart-to-hearts, but with Lexi, things are different. She stops, too, turning to face me in the soft glow of the distant streetlights.

"Everything okay?" she asks, her brow furrowed in concern.

I run a hand through my hair, a nervous habit I can't seem to shake. "There's something I've been meaning to talk to you about." My voice is more serious than before, and I watch her expression shift to match my tone.

"Shoot." She tucks a strand of sandy blonde hair behind her ear, giving me her full attention.

"I've been thinking about what you said earlier... about being there for me, with my family stuff."

She stops and turns to face me, her expression open and attentive. "Yeah?"

"What about being there for me in…other aspects."

She looks momentarily confused.

"Like...?" she prods, brows furrowing ever so slightly.

A rush of adrenaline causes my heart to thump wildly in my chest. This is it. My chance to voice the feelings that have been grumbling like an undercurrent within me for some time now.

"Like as my girlfriend," I blurt out, surprising myself with the raw honesty in my voice. I know my statement is abrupt and awkward at best, but I can't seem to find a smoother way to say it. My gaze flicks up to meet hers, searching her face for a reaction, a hint of what she might say next.

The silence stretches between us as she takes a moment to process my words. But then, she's smiling - a slow, radiant smile that outshines any star in the night sky. It radiates warmth, softness, the promise of shared laughter and whispered dreams. A sense of relief washes over me, and I can't help but let out a shaky laugh.

"Wes Jacobs," she says, her voice full of that infectious laughter of hers, "are you asking me to be your girlfriend?"

"Um... yeah. Yeah, I am." I feel my cheeks flush a bit in embarrassment, but I don't look away from her gaze.

She looks thoughtful for a moment, her eyes glinting with a spark of mischief, before she finally says, "Yeah. Yeah, I think I'd like that."

A weight I didn't know I was carrying lifts from my shoulders. With a rush of unadulterated exhilaration, I pull her into my arms and kiss her there beneath the stars. Her lips are soft and warm against mine. The kiss is everything — sweet and heated, full of promise — matching the rapid beat of my heart. She wraps her arms tight around my neck, holding me close, her laughter vibrating against my chest as we break apart.

"Wow," she breathes out, her cheeks flushed.

My heart's pounding like it's got its own set of drums, and Lexi's pressed against me, a perfect fit. We're in the shadowed corner of two campus buildings, just a breath away from the window where the moonlight spills in, casting a silver glow on her face. I can see the flecks of gold in her green eyes, wild and fixed on mine.

"Are you sure?" My voice is rough, almost a whisper, because this—us—it's new territory, and I want to be certain she's with me every step of the way.

"Absolutely," she breathes out, and there's no hesitation, just that fierce independence I admire so much. Her hands roam over my chest, finding their way under my shirt, tracing the lines of muscle I've earned on the ice. The sensation sends a jolt straight through me, leaving a trail of heat in its wake.

I lean down, capturing her lips with mine again, and she meets me with equal fervor. It's a kiss that seals promises and whispers secrets, a collision of everything we've been holding back. Her fingers tangle in my hair, pulling me closer, and I oblige, deepening the kiss until there's nowhere else to go but further into each other.

"God, Wes," she gasps when we finally break for air, and her voice is laced with so much more than desire; there's trust, there's raw emotion, there's the beginning of something neither of us can quite name yet.

But then my phone rings, shattering the moment, a harsh buzz that feels like a bucket of ice water. I ignore it, desperate to keep Lexi close, to stay wrapped up in the world we're creating just for us.

"Leave it," she murmurs against my neck, and I'm about to do just that when it rings again, persistent and demanding.

I pull away, reluctantly, and check the caller ID. Mom. This late at night, it can only mean trouble. I swipe to answer, pressing the phone to my ear.

"Mom? What's wrong?" My voice sounds foreign, strained with concern that I know Lexi can hear. A knot forms in my stomach, tight and foreboding.

"Weston," she gasps between breaths, her voice quivering like a leaf in the wind, "the doctor says... the chemo isn't working still. They want to go more aggressive, but—"

"Okay, okay," I say quickly, pressing the phone tighter against my ear as if proximity could bridge the gap between comforting words and her reality. "Let's not panic, all right? We've got options. There are always new treatments to try." I'm speaking in the calm, assured tone that has become second nature whenever these calls come, but the echo of desperation never quite leaves my voice.

"Everything feels like it's falling apart," she whispers, the sound of her fear slicing through me more sharply than any skate blade ever could.

"Hey, remember when the Zamboni broke down mid-game my senior year of high school, and we all thought the night was ruined?" I start, conjuring up the memory of absurdity rather than despair. "But then Coach just had us play street hockey in the parking lot until they fixed it. We adapt, okay? We're Jacobs. We don't break; we bend, and we keep playing, no matter what."

There's a pause, a hiccup of hope in the silence, and I imagine her nodding, gripping the phone like a lifeline. "You always know just what to say to make me smile, even now."

"Of course, I do," I say with a chuckle that doesn't quite sound genuine. "I'm your son, remember? Now, let's talk about what's next. We're in this game together, remember?" I lean back against the wall, feeling the cold seep through my jacket, a stark reminder of the chill settling into my bones that has nothing to do with the weather.

My thumb presses hard against the phone's edge, and I angle my body subtly, trying to create a barrier between Lexi and the trembling voice spilling out of the speaker. She's too close, and it's like my mom's fear is this tangible thing that could reach out and claw at her. I can't let that happen.

"Listen, Mom," I say, keeping my voice steady, "I'm gonna tell you a story, all right? Picture this: It's the championship game, that same game senior year, we're down by one, and the puck's coming at me. What do I do?"

"Score," she responds with a frail attempt at cheer, her voice shaky.

"Exactly," I reply. "Because we never lose hope, even when the clock's running out. We play harder, fight smarter."

I sneak a glance at Lexi, who's pretending to check her phone, giving us the illusion of privacy. But I know she's listening; she's got that crinkle between her brows she gets when she's concerned.

"Remember how I used to shoot pucks in the garage for hours?" I continue, hoping the nostalgia might ground her. "Well, every shot was practice for moments like these. Life's throwing curveballs, but we've been training for this our whole lives, right?"

"Right," she whispers, steadier now, and I imagine her sitting up straighter, the fighter in her reignited.

"Good," I nod, even though she can't see me. "So, we're going to approach this next round of treatments like it's overtime. We'll give it everything we've got, leave nothing on the table. You with me?"

"Overtime," she repeats, a spark of her old tenacity flickering. "I'm with you."

"Great. Hang tight, Mom. I want to talk to a friend, and then I'll call you back in a bit with a game plan." I end the call and finally look at Lexi, who looks full of questions. But for now, they'll have to wait.

I pocket my phone, the weight of the call still pressing against my chest. I can feel Lexi's gaze on me, her concern almost tangible. She doesn't say anything, just watches me, seeming to see right through the armor I wear in front of everyone else.

"Your mom?" she asks softly, and I nod. It's all I manage before the lump in my throat threatens to choke me.

Lexi steps closer, her presence a calming force. She's seen me at my best on the ice, but now she's witnessing the cracks in my game face. I catch the admiration in her expression when she thinks I'm not looking—admiration for handling a call that would knock anyone else off their skates.

"Should... should I go back home?" I ask the question more to myself than to her, my voice barely above a whisper. The thought is like a puck to the gut, sending a jolt of cold fear through me. But it's what you do, isn't it? When your team—no, when your family—is down, you don't just skate away.

"Is she alone?" Lexi's practicality cuts through the chaos of my emotions.

"Yeah," I admit, raking a hand through my hair. "And she's scared. I mean, who wouldn't be?"

"Then that's where you start," she says firmly, her own experience with injury giving her a coach-like authority. "Figure out what support she has, then decide your next move. You're the king of strategy on the ice, Wes. Use that off the ice, too."

She's right. My mind works best when I'm strategizing plays, anticipating the opponent's next move—so why not apply that to real life? I pull out my phone again, ready to dial my mom back.

"Hey, it's me again," I say when she answers. "I've been thinking... Do you need me to come home?"

"Because I will, Mom. In a heartbeat."

"Stay where you are, Wes," Mom's voice comes through the phone, firm despite the tremors of fear I heard just moments ago. "You've got a scholarship to think about, and your team needs you."

"But, Mom—" I start, the protest lodged in my throat like a puck stuck against the boards.

"No buts. I didn't raise my boy to drop his stick mid-game," she cuts me off, that familiar maternal determination seeping through the crackling connection. "You're doing so well, and I'm not going to be the reason you lose sight of your goals."

I pace the length of my cramped dorm room, passing Lexi with each turn. She watches silently, her presence a steady comfort. "You managed fine as a single mother," I concede, trying to keep the worry from my voice but failing. "But this is different, it's serious."

"We've faced off against harder times, haven't we?" she counters, and I can almost hear the smile in her voice, brave and unyielding.

"Yeah, we have," I admit, knowing full well the resilience that runs in our veins. But this time, my fear for her is a heavy weight on my chest, like I've just blocked a slap shot with no padding.

"Promise me something, then," she says, and I nod before realizing she can't see it.

"Anything," I say, and it's a vow, as solemn as any I've made on the ice.

"Promise you'll focus on your classes—and hockey." There's a gentle sternness to her words, the kind of tone that's always guided me through tough decisions.

"Okay, I promise," I agree reluctantly, feeling the fight go out of me. But there's one play left in my strategy, a line shift I can make from a distance. "Listen, I'm setting up a grocery delivery for you. It'll be there tomorrow. And Mrs. Kowalski next door, I'm texting her to check in on you, all right?"

"Fine, fine," she concedes, and I imagine her rolling her eyes, though with gratitude rather than irritation. "Just don't make a fuss."

"Me? Make a fuss?" I quip, attempting to inject some levity into the conversation. A small chuckle escapes her, and I feel a tiny victory amidst the uncertainty.

"Take care of yourself, Mom," I insist, the sincerity in my voice as clear as the cling of skates on fresh ice. "That's an order."

"All right," she replies, her voice soft but filled with love that spans the miles between us. "I will."

The call ends, and suddenly the dorm room feels too silent, too still. My gaze drifts to Lexi, her expression reflecting both concern and admiration—a mix that stirs something warm inside me, even as the rest of me grapples with helplessness.

9 - 10

I thumb the end call button, but before I can pull the phone away from my ear, her voice comes through again, fragile as thin ice.

"Before you go, Wes...are you okay?"

"Sure, Mom, I'm good," I reply, trying to keep my voice steady.

"Are you...lonely there?" Her question hangs between us, laden with concern.

My eyes flick to Lexi, who's leaning against my desk, arms crossed over her chest, her jersey hugging her shoulders like a battle standard. A silent strength emanates from her, grounding me. "No, not lonely." But I can't bring myself to tell my mom about us, not now. The words feel too heavy, too real for this fragile moment.

"All right. Take care of yourself, honey."

"Will do, Mom." I hang up and tuck the phone back into my coat pocket. It hangs with a soft weight, echoing the sudden weight in my chest.

Lexi pushes off from the wall opposite me and walks towards me, her movements graceful, deliberate. She doesn't say anything, just reaches out and takes my hand, intertwining our fingers. There's a strength to her grip, a testament to hours spent taping sticks and carrying equipment. It's reassuring, solid.

"Hey," she says, her voice gentle, her thumb brushing against the back of my hand. "You're the strongest person I know, Wes Jacobs. But even strong solo players need a team, you know?"

Her words chip away at the ice wall I've built around myself, and a half-laugh, half-sigh escapes me. "Guess that makes you my MVP, Turner."

She smiles, that deep-dimpled grin that first knocked the breath out of me on the rink sidelines. "Always. You set them up; I'll knock them down."

"Promise?" I ask, only half-joking.

"Promise," she confirms, and something in her tone tells me she's not just talking about hypothetical hockey assists.

"Thanks, Lex," I murmur, squeezing her hand. In the cold, crisp air, we've found a quiet corner of the world where panic and worry can't reach me. Just for now, just with her.

"Anytime, Wes," she whispers back, her gaze holding mine as if she's memorizing the play before the puck drops. "Anytime."

I look at Lexi Turner, and my heart squeezes in my chest. I have no idea what we're really doing—but I'm not going to let her out of my sight, out of reach of my arms and lips, until we figure out what this new connection means.

CHAPTER FOURTEEN: NOAH

The clock's relentless ticking echoes in my head—a constant reminder of the long hours that have morphed into a rote routine. I've become all too familiar with the crushing weight of responsibility that rests on my shoulders as we've won game after game this season—we're hovering near a championship now. It's not just about the game anymore; it's about proving myself worthy of the letter 'C' emblazoned on my jersey.

I glide across the ice, the chill biting at my cheeks, the sharp scrape of my skates against the rink a symphony to my ears. Practice has become my sanctuary, a place where the pressure simmers down to a dull roar and my focus narrows to the puck at my stick. Drenched in sweat beneath layers of padding, I zigzag through drills, each stride fueled by sheer determination. The sting of exhaustion gnaws at my muscles, but I push harder, faster, because slowing down isn't an option—not when every pass, every shot counts.

I ignore the ache in my ankle—Wes is right. It's easy once you're used to it.

"Keep up, Captain!" one of the rookies calls out, his voice teasing. I toss him a grin—half cocky, half encouraging—and fire off a pass that lands tape-to-tape on his stick.

"Nice shot, Bishop!" comes another shout from the bench. Coach Thompson.

"Thanks, but save the cheers for the game," I shoot back, my breath coming out in visible puffs.

My smile might be easy, but there's nothing casual about the way my heart hammers against my ribcage. Each practice is a battle against my own limits, and I relish the fight, even as my body screams for mercy. This is what it means to lead—to set the pace and never show any sign of weakness. I see Wes skating circles around me all morning, and I saw him leave with Lexi last night. Even today, they keep going off to the side, putting their heads together in secret little talks. He doesn't look at all injured, at all weak. In fact, he looks like a winner.

"All right, boys, bring it in!" Coach bellows, clapping his hands to signal the end of practice.

We huddle together, a mass of adrenaline and ambition, our breaths mingling in the frosty air. I'm right in the middle, where I need to be, ready to lift spirits or crack a joke when the tension gets too thick. I avoid looking at Wes, though.

"Listen up," I start, my voice cutting through the cold. "We're only as strong as we are united. Let's take this energy and bottle it up for the next match."

A chorus of sticks banging against the ice greets my words—a resounding affirmation that they're with me, that we're in this together. It's moments like these that make the long hours and sleepless nights worth it. And as we disband, I skate off the ice, the heaviness of my role as captain eclipsed by the lightness of being part of a family—a team that plays and fights as one.

***

The air in the locker room is electric, each breath a crackle of pure anticipation. We're on the cusp of something monumental, the kind of game that gets etched into memory and replayed in slow motion during restless nights. It's us versus them – the age-old clash with the Highlanders, our rivals who've tasted victory one too many times for my liking. But not this time; we've come too far, worked too hard.

"Biggest game of the season tonight, boys!" Dean slaps his stick against the bench, his grin all confidence and swagger. "Time to show those Highlanders what real hockey looks like."

The stakes are sky-high: win and we cement our lossless legacy, lose and it's a year of what-ifs. We rewrite history.

"Let's make 'em wish they never stepped onto the ice," I add, my voice steady, strong.

The team erupts in cheers, the sound a battle cry that fills the room with unshakable resolve. I grab my helmet, ready to lead the charge, when it happens – a sharp twist, a misstep as I rise from the bench. Pain explodes in my ankle, white-hot and searing. For a moment, I see nothing but blinding light against my eyelids.

"Captain down!" someone calls out, half-joking until they see my face contorted in pain.

"Shake it off, Bishop," Coach says, but his smirk has faded, replaced by concern.

I try to stand, testing my weight on the injured ankle, but it's no use. The pain is a vice, tightening with every movement. Emotions churn within me, frustration and fear mingling in a bitter cocktail. I can't be sidelined, not now, not when everything we've worked for hangs in the balance.

"Damn it," I hiss through clenched teeth, slamming a fist against the bench. The echo rings louder than any cheer, a stark reminder of my sudden vulnerability.

"Easy, Noah," Coach kneels beside me, his seasoned eyes assessing the situation. "We need you."

"Coach, I can play through it," I assure, the words a lifeline I'm desperate to believe.

He gives me a look, one that says he's heard that line before, from players who didn't know when to back down. But I'm different, I want to tell him. I have to be.

"Let's get that checked out first," he says, firm yet not unkind. "But I would say it’s best if you can tough it out for the greater good."

Greater good... The words sting more than the injury. It's a test of wills, my heart battling my head, the desire to push through the pain clashing with the responsibility I have to the team, to myself. As they help me up, I'm struck by the weight of what lies ahead – a pivotal game that could slip through our fingers, and the realization that sometimes being a leader means bearing the pain. I won't give up. Not yet. There's still time before the puck drops, time to face this head-on and emerge victorious. After all, isn't that what captains do?

***

Tape hisses as it wraps tightly around my ankle, a firm grip steadying my heel. Lexi's skilled fingers move with precision, deft and sure as she secures the bandage, her touch professional but not without compassion. I wince, not from the pain – which is there, throbbing insistently – but from the realization that under her gentleness, she’s, well, mad.

"Keep still, Noah," Lexi chides gently, focused intently on the task at hand. Her ponytail sways as she leans in closer, assessing her work. "You need this to be stabilized properly if you're going to stand a chance out there."

"Thanks, Doc," I say, trying to keep the mood light despite the weight of worry settling in my chest. The locker room feels colder now, the buzz of anticipation for the game ahead overshadowed by the dull ache of my injury.

"Ha, not a doctor yet," she says, flashing me a grin that doesn't quite reach her eyes. I can tell she's concerned, maybe more than she's letting on. There's a diligence in her movements, a quiet intensity that speaks volumes about her dedication. She's seen injuries like mine before, knows the risks and the stakes.

"Could've fooled me." I attempt a smile, hoping to mask the mix of gratitude and something else – something warmer, more dangerous – that flares up whenever she's near. Lexi's whip-smart, fiercely independent, and yeah, easy on the eyes too. Not that I'd ever admit that out loud. Not now, not with Cassidy and I…dating?

"Flattery will get you nowhere," she retorts, but there's a hint of playfulness in her voice. "Especially not back on the ice faster."

"Can't blame a guy for trying," I counter, watching her as she packs away her medical supplies.

"Try focusing on recovery instead." She stands, crossing her arms over her chest, her jersey fitting snugly over her athletic build. "And don't even think about pushing yourself too hard, got it?"

"Got it," I reply, though we both know I'm terrible at following orders when it comes to sitting out. Especially not when Wes pushes through. But Lexi, she's got this way of making me want to listen, to actually consider that maybe the smart play isn't always the most reckless one.

"Good." She nods, satisfied, turning away.

I wince as I shift my weight, the motion pulling at the tender skin around the bandage. Across the room, Lexi's back is to me, her attention on restocking the medical supplies. The silence between us isn't awkward—not exactly. It's thick with words we're not saying, heavy with a tension that feels like it's more than just concern for my sprained ankle.

"Hey, Lexi?" My voice breaks the stillness, and she turns, those piercing green eyes locking onto mine. "Do you think... I mean, how bad do you reckon this is? Honestly?"

She strides over, her movements efficient and sure, the very image of professionalism. But I see the way her brow furrows, the slight bite of her lower lip, and I know she's worried. For the game or about me, I can't tell.

"Your ankle will heal, Noah," she says as she takes a seat next to me, her tone matter-of-fact but not unkind. "And I—I think Thompson is wrong to be pushing you like this. You don't have to say it. I know he's ignoring what Drew recommends, what I'd recommend. But you need to take it seriously. No messing around, okay?"

I nod, trying to digest her words while battling the urge to reach out, to bridge the gap between professional concern and personal care. "I get it. I just—"

"Just what?" Her head tilts inquisitively, and I'm caught in her gaze, wanting to dive into the depths of whatever we're skirting around.

"Nothing," I manage, forcing a laugh that sounds more hollow than humorous. "Just gotta make sure I'm ready for the match, right?"

"Right." She doesn't smile, though. Instead, she studies me, and I feel like she's reading every page of the book I didn't realize I'd been writing. "You're pushing yourself too hard, Noah. This isn't just about the game."

"Isn't it?" I challenge, but even to my own ears, it sounds defensive. I am the captain. The team relies on me. And yet, here I am, unsure if I'm fighting for the win or for something else entirely.

"Sometimes I wonder if you remember how to be anything other than Captain Bishop," Lexi murmurs, and her words sting like an accurate slapshot.

"Maybe I don't want to," I admit softly, half to myself. The confession hangs in the air.

"Everyone needs a break, Noah. Even you." Her hand hovers near mine, not touching, but the warmth radiates across the small space.

Lexi helps me up, her hand steadying my elbow as I test my weight on the injured leg. Moments later, the rink's cold seeps into my bones, a chill that's more than just physical—it's anticipation, fear, adrenaline. It's playoff season, and every shift on the ice counts. Coach Thompson is rinkside, watching us like a hawk.

"Let's see you skate," she says, and there's an edge to her voice that's new. Worry, maybe, or frustration. With me? With the situation? With Thompson? Hard to tell.

I don't see Drew. He was here at the start, but now, where did he run off to?

I push off, gliding across the ice, the familiar scrape and hiss of blade on rink drowning out everything else. Each stride sends a jolt up my leg, but I keep going, faster, harder. If I can feel the pain, it means I'm still in this fight.

"Looking good, Bishop!" Coach calls out. His approval comes with a wink—a silent acknowledgment of the unspoken code among players: Hide your weaknesses, play till you drop.

"Take a break, Noah!" Lexi shouts from the bench, but I shake my head. There's no time for breaks, not when the championship is on the line.

The rest of practice blurs—a series of drills, shots, checks—each one a battle between my body's protests and my mind's stubborn refusal to yield. Lexi watches, her brow furrowed, clipboard clutched like a shield. She's scribbling notes, no doubt planning my rehab schedule down to the minute.

"Enough," Coach finally says, stepping onto the ice, whistle around his neck unheard above the din. "You're done for today, boys."

I want to argue, to claim I can handle more, but I nod, conceding this round, and skate off the ice.

CHAPTER FIFTEEN: LEXI

The chill from the ice rink seeps into my bones at morning practice, but it's nothing against the warmth that spreads through me when I think of Wes. As I watch him skate across the ice, a rebel in skates, my heart does that familiar leap-and-twirl. It's like he's performing just for me, each pivot and glide a secret dance we share.

I lean against the cold barrier, scribbling notes on my clipboard, pretending to focus on the players, injuries, but my mind wanders back to the late-night conversations, the cozy coffee dates, the way he listens, really listens, when I talk about my fears and hopes. And the way he'd calmed his mom down the night she'd called, feeling sick and panicked. He might not be the med student, but he's definitely a caregiver—a side of him he doesn't show many.

"Turner!" Coach yells, snapping me back to reality. "Stay sharp!"

"Got it, Coach," I call back, forcing my gaze away from Wes and back to the task at hand. Coach Thomspon makes me nervous now, and as I monitor the players, checking for signs of strain or injury, my pulse races with adrenaline. Drew and Thomspon had…words at practice, and Drew stormed off. I haven't seen him in two days.

My phone buzzes in my jacket pocket, an email alert. I turn my back on Coach Thompson and swipe to read it, and suddenly, my chest tightens. Another internship offer—at an Illinois hospital, one known for its cutting-edge sports medicine program.

No way. I'd applied to this program a year ago, and had heard crickets. It's why I'd ended up with the Aces, though I now believed that this was where fate had placed me. But the hospital position, it's an opportunity that could catapult me straight into the career I've been dreaming of since I traded my own skates for textbooks and physiotherapy bands.

I picture myself walking those sterile corridors, learning from the best, helping athletes recover and return to the sports they love. It's everything I've worked toward, every extra credit, every volunteer hour spent shadowing tired yet passionate professionals—it's all led to this moment. Excitement bubbles up like a well-aimed slap shot, making me want to shout my news to the world. This is big—bigger than any game-winning goal or championship title. This is my future calling.

Isn’t it?

"Lexi!" Wes skates over now, practice finished, helmet off, revealing that trademark tousled hair. I bite my lip, anticipation mingling with nerves. How will he react? Will he be proud? Or will the distance this internship puts between us cool the heat we've kindled?

"Great practice, huh?" he says, grinning, unaware of the storm of emotions behind my smile.

"Absolutely," I agree, because right now, in this frozen moment, everything is perfect. We're just Lexi and Wes, two college kids laughing on an ice rink, blissfully ignorant of the choices looming ahead.

"Can't wait to take you to lunch," he adds, leaning on the barrier close enough for me to catch the scent of his cologne mixed with the freshness of the ice. “You have a break around one?”

"I do," I say, the words heavy. I need advice—stat.

***

I stride into the dorm I share with Jenna, my heart thrumming faster than my feet on the pavement after a long run. The lingering chill from the rink still clings to my skin, but it's the heat of opportunity that has me all fired up inside.

"Guess who just got an internship offer at one of the top hospitals?" I announce before Jenna can even get a word in edgewise.

She looks up from her biology textbook, eyebrows hitting the ceiling. "No way! That's amazing, Lexi!" She tosses his highlighter onto the table and leans back. "Tell me everything!"

As I recount the details, her grin mirrors the excitement I feel bubbling in my chest. But as quickly as it comes, a shadow passes over me, dimming the brightness of the moment. It's the same shadow that's been following me around since I got the offer.

"Hey, what's up?" Jenna senses the shift in my mood. "You look like you just lost your favorite finger splint."

I sigh and drop onto the couch beside her, tucking my feet under me. "It's Wes," I confess, the words tumbling out like loose pucks on ice. "This internship is in Chicago. If I take it, it means long distance... and Wes and I—"

"Are pretty hot and heavy right now," Jenna finishes for me, waggling her eyebrows comically. "But come on, Lexi. This is your dream we're talking about."

"Exactly." I run a hand through my hair, feeling the familiar tug of my ponytail. "I've wanted this forever. But falling for Wes wasn't part of the plan. I'm scared that choosing the internship means losing him."

"Look, I might not be the expert on romances," Jenna says, scratching her head, "but isn't Wes Mr. 'Live-for-the-moment'? Maybe he'd understand more than you think."

"Maybe," I murmur, though doubt gnaws at me. Wes lives for the adrenaline rush, the here and now; I'm not sure if our relationship can survive the test of time and distance.

"Besides, Lexi, you can't make career choices based on a guy." Jenna's tone is gentle but firm. "Especially a rebellious hockey player who probably has half his life planned out on napkins."

"Harsh," I shoot back half-heartedly, knowing there's truth in her words. Wes has always been a wild card, but isn't that part of his allure?

"Think about it," she continues. "You're smart, ambitious, and you've got a killer slap shot with medical jargon. You can't give up on your dreams for someone else—no matter how chiseled his jawline is."

"Or how deep his blue eyes are," I add with a weak smile.

"Exactly. You need to do what's best for you, Lexi. Besides, who knows? Maybe a little distance will bring you closer together in the end. Or maybe it'll clear the rink for something else that's meant to be."

"Thanks, Jenna," I say, a genuine smile breaking through. I stand up, feeling a little lighter but still carrying the weight of the decision.

"Anytime," she replies, picking up her highlighter. "Now go talk to Wes. See where he stands."

"Right." My stomach does a nervous loop-de-loop. Talking to Wes. That's the next move. And suddenly, I feel like I'm facing a shootout with the stakes higher than any game I've ever played.

CHAPTER SIXTEEN: NOAH

I'm tapping my stick against the boards in a steady rhythm, a habit I've picked up when I'm deep in thought. Each tap echoes the cadence of my heartbeat, which seems to spike every single time Lexi flashes across my thoughts—the way she lights up when she talks about hockey, or how her laugh sounds like the perfect melody after a game-winning goal. Lexi Turner isn't just any girl; she's become the axis on which my world spins, and that terrifies me.

Cassidy has noticed—in fact, she's ignoring my calls at the moment because of it. Not that I could have taken a return call. I've spent the last two hours on the phone with my dad, and there's a new complication in life. One that makes it imperative that The Aces win the championships this year.

"Hey, Noah, you going to practice that puck handling, or are you planning on serenading the ice with your stick all day?" Dean quips as he sails by, breaking my trance.

"Very funny, Hartley," I shoot back, trying to plaster over my internal chaos with a smirk. But his words don't sting as much today because my head's too full of Lexi and what might be slipping through my fingers. And of what my dad had said today.

Son, the farm's too much to handle on our own. No good help to be found. If hockey doesn't work out this year, you've got to come home...

My mind if a jumbled mess, and I just want to talk to Lexi. We've shared moments that felt so intense, they could melt this very ice—and it's those fragments of time that linger with me, heavy with what-ifs and could-bes. But Wes...he's a force to be reckoned with, not just on the ice but in the messy game of emotions as well. The guy's got this magnetic pull that even I can't deny—and Lexi's caught right in the middle. Every time I see them together, something tightens in my chest, a cold fist that clenches with the fear of losing her to him.

Moreover, I'm afraid that I'm about to lose my very place here, at school.

But if my family needs me...

Then, as if I've conjured her, she's here—across the rink, searching the arena. My hands shove into the pockets of my jeans, curling into fists around nothing. I stand up, setting my stick aside.

"Lexi," I call out before I can stop myself. She turns, and something about the way she looks at me—expectant, a little hopeful—has words tumbling from my lips before I can think better of them. "Can we talk?"

"Sure." She jogs around the rink to me. Her voice is guarded, and I'm suddenly aware of every inch of space between us, itching to close the distance but rooted to the spot by the weight of what I'm about to say.

"Have you seen Wes?" she asks, and it makes my gut twist.

Tell her.

I have to know if there's even a chance. If not, maybe the farm's my fate. Or maybe I can play with her at rinkside without feeling my heart in my throat, as long as there's closure.

"No. Listen, I just... need you to know something." I draw in a breath, steeling myself against the vulnerability, clawing its way up my throat. "This thing between us, it's been more than just..." I trail off, struggling to put into words emotions that feel too big for any language.

"More than just what?" she prompts, tilting her head slightly, the movement sending a ripple through me.

"More than just teammates, more than just friends." I lock eyes with her, letting the truth of it shine through.

Her brows furrow, confusion and maybe a flicker of something else crossing her features. I push on, even as my heart thuds a frantic rhythm against my ribs.

"Look, I know Wes is... he's in the picture," I say, the name tasting like stale coffee on my tongue. "And I get it, I do. He's got this way about him that draws people in. But I'd be lying through my teeth if I said it didn't scare the hell out of me—the thought of losing a chance with you to him."

"Is this you trying to make a play, Noah Bishop?" Lexi's attempt at lightness doesn't quite mask the tremor in her voice.

"It's me being honest." I take a step closer, driven by a force I can't name. "It's me saying that whatever decision you make about... us, I want it to be yours. Fully and completely. But I also want you to know that you mean more to me than just a line on a roster or a partner in practice drills."

"More to me, too," she whispers, and hope flares bright and hot in my chest.

"Good, because..." I pause, swallowing past the sudden tightness in my throat. "Because I'm pretty sure I've fallen for you, Lexi Turner. And damn if that isn't the most terrifying and best feeling I've ever had."

There's a beat of silence, the kind that stretches out long enough to make me second guess every word that's just left my mouth. But then she steps into my space, closing the gap until I can feel the warmth radiating from her.

"Your timing could use some work, Captain," she says with a shaky laugh, but there's no mistaking the sincerity in her eyes. "But I can't say I haven't felt it too—the pull, the connection. It's just..." Her gaze drops to where her fingers are absently playing with the hem of her jersey.

"Complicated," I finish for her, and she nods.

"Complicated," she echoes.

“What about Cassidy?” she asks.

I smile. “It’s complicated.”

My hand lifts, almost of its own accord, to tuck a loose strand of hair behind her ear. "I don't need easy, Lex. I just need real. Whatever that looks like."

"Real." She tests the word. Her eyes search mine, looking for any sign of insincerity. I make sure she finds none. "You're a good man, Noah Bishop. Too good for your own good sometimes," she says with a small, wry smile.

"Maybe," I concede, the corner of my mouth ticking up despite the ache in my heart. "But I meant what I said earlier about needing real. This—talking to you, being honest even when it hurts—that's as real as it gets for me."

“And if I’m being honest, my mind is on something else—something possibly life-changing—that’s not a romance-related decision. And you have the game tonight. Can we…can we put this on the back burner for now?”

I nod, but I can’t put the thought of her decision out of my head. Because no matter how tonight’s game ends, it's the one off the ice that has the highest stakes—the one for Lexi's heart. And that's a game I'm playing for keeps.

CHAPTER SEVENTEEN: WES

My skates cut through the ice, a sharp contrast to the turmoil that's anything but smooth in my head. Missed calls and texts while I'd been in class earlier had led to a rushed meet with Lexi between classes, and I her news. The internship offer—it's a game-changer, not just for her career but for whatever it is that's been sparking between us. Part of me wants to drop the gloves and fight for her to stay, but I know that's not fair. She's got dreams bigger than this rink, and I'd be a real goon to hold her back.

I'd skipped my last class to have the rink to myself.

I flick the puck hard across the ice, watching it slam against the boards with a satisfying crack. Hockey's always been my escape, the one place where life's complications don't penetrate the ice. But even here, Lexi's dilemma follows me.

She's everything I never knew I wanted—fierce, independent, and as passionate about hockey as I am. Her laugh punches through the ambient noise of the locker room, even though she's not here. It's just a memory, a replay of one of our many verbal spars that always seems to end with her smile triumphing over my sarcasm.

"Yo, Jacobs! You hitting the bar tonight?" Dean Hartley hoots and hollers after the question, breaking my reverie with his usual lack of subtlety.

"Maybe," I grunt, not really in the mood for the playboy winger's brand of nightlife. What are he and the rookies doing here, anyway?

"Come on, man, you need to loosen up. Forget about whatever chick's got you wound up."

He's skating on thin ice, bringing up my personal life, especially when he has no clue who's in my head. But I let it slide. "We'll see," I say, shrugging him off and ignoring them until they all leave the arena, loud and boisterous.

I'm out the door before anyone else can show up and try to pry. The evening air bites at my skin, a reminder that winter's not done with us yet. I shove my hands into my pockets and start the walk back to my dorm. It's nothing fancy, but it's mine—a place where I can shut the door and pretend, just for a little while, that I've got everything figured out.

The streets are busy with students, all caught up in their own dramas and deadlines. I keep my gaze fixed ahead, dodging bodies like they're rival defensemen trying to check me. By the time I reach my front door, I've managed to convince myself that I'm focused on the next game, that Lexi's choice is hers alone and whatever happens, happens.

But who am I kidding? As I turn the key and step inside, I know I'm just biding time until I have to face her decision—and what it means for us—head-on.

The door to my apartment is up ahead, and there she stands—Lexi Turner in the flesh, looking like she's about to face off in the most crucial game of her life. Her whole demeanor suggests this isn't a casual visit.

"Hey," she says, and I can hear the edge in her voice. It's sharp enough to skate on.

"Lexi." I unlock the door, gesturing for her to come in. "C'mon."

She takes a deep breath as she enters, surveying my modest living space like she's strategizing her next play. When she finally turns to face me, her expression is serious, a stark contrast to the playful banter that usually defines our interactions.

"I've been doing some thinking," she begins, folding her arms over her chest defensively. "About the internship."

I lean against the wall, trying to appear relaxed even though my heart's pounding like it's overtime and we're one goal down. "Okay."

"It's in Chicago, Wes," Lexi says, as if I could've forgotten. "That's not just a weekend trip away. And after we graduate, you'll be working, presumably, and so will I—in addition to starting the new internship. It's going to be a lot of work."

I can't help but admire her, standing there all fired up about her future. But it's the 'more' that tightens something inside my chest.

"It's not that far. But, Lexi, you don't have to explain. I get it. It's an amazing opportunity."

"Is that it, then? Just... 'good luck, see you when I see you'?" There's a tremor in her voice now, one she's fighting hard to control.

"Of course not," I reply quickly. "You know I'm proud of you, right? You're going to do great things."

"Stop, Wes," she cuts in, shaking her head. "I need to know what this means for us. For whatever this is between us," she adds, gesturing vaguely in the space between us.

I push off from the wall, closing the distance. "I want you to go. You deserve this."

"But?"

"But nothing. I mean, sure, it scares the crap out of me—the thought of you being so far away. But that's my problem, not yours."

"Scared?" Lexi arches an eyebrow, a ghost of her usual humor flickering there. "Wes Jacobs, afraid of a little distance?"

"Hey, I never said I was invincible," I quip back, trying to break the tension.

"Good, because you're not Superman. And I'm definitely not Lois Lane waiting to be saved," she retorts, but the smile doesn't quite reach her eyes this time.

"Look, Lexi," I say, taking another step closer. "I don't know what the playbook says about long-distance relationships or how to be the perfect boyfriend while you're out there kicking ass at your internship. But I do know that I don't want to hold you back."

"Who says you're holding me back?" she challenges, her gaze softening just a bit.

"Nobody. I just—I don't want you to leave with any doubts. About me. About us."

"Even if it means I'll be in another city?" Her voice is soft, but there's a steel edge to it, the same one she uses when she's fighting for an injured player to get more recovery time.

"Even if." I nod, because what else can I do? Love her and let her go, or love her and hold her back? Not much of a choice. "We'll work through it, Lexi. Calls, texts, visits whenever we can swing it."

"Really?"

There's hope there, and something clenches in my chest. *Yeah, really.*

"Really. I want you to chase down every last dream you've got. And I'll be here, cheering you on the loudest." I mean every word, and I hope she hears that, too. I want her to soar, even if it means I'm watching from the ground.

"Thanks, Wes. That... that means everything." She steps closer, and I can't help but reach out, fingers brushing against hers. Solid, strong, capable—just like her.

I reach for her hand, our fingers intertwining with an ease that's become second nature. Lexi squeezes back, a silent acknowledgment of the whirlwind encircling us. We're standing in the midst of our own personal crossroads, her potential departure hanging in the air like the last stubborn leaf clinging to a winter branch.

"Hey," I say softly, thumb brushing over her knuckles, "come here."

Lexi steps closer, and I pull her into my arms, our bodies fitting together as perfectly as the final pieces of a puzzle. The warmth of her seeps into me, grounding me despite the chaos of my racing thoughts. It's moments like these—her head resting against my chest, my chin atop her hair—that I realize how much I've come to rely on her presence.

"Wes," she whispers. "There's something else…"

I tense. What else could she possibly have to tell me? The moment feels settled. I pull back slightly to look into her eyes, which are troubled.

"Yeah?"

"Noah…" she starts, but then stops.

"What about Noah?" I frown, waiting.

She sighs, long and deep. "He, uh"—she seems to gather herself—"I'm not sure his ankle will hold at the game. But Coach is really pushing him."

I relax. *Is that all?*

"Don't worry about it. He has us, his team. He has you. We won't let anything happen to him."

She nods, pressing her lips together in a slim line, before forcing a small smile. It doesn't quite reach her eyes, and I sense an undercurrent of tension that wasn't there before. Something is off.

"All right," she says quietly, meeting my gaze with a seriousness that thrums doubt into my veins.

I wrap my arms around her waist tighter, pulling her closer until she's nestled against me once more. The beat of her heart echoes in sync with mine, a steady rhythm that brings an odd sort of comfort amidst what feels like a brewing storm.

CHAPTER EIGHTEEN: LEXI

I don't want to do this—observe the Ace-ettes Cheer practice. I want to be in bed, hiding under my covers, trying to sort out the mess that is Wes and the internship and Noah and his confession. But here I am, stuck in the gymnasium, the scent of polished wood and sweat greeting me like an old teammate's slapshot. Coach Thompson is keeping me away from the players in the final practice before the playoffs. I would be a fool not to notice,

So, it's cheer practice, and I'm here under the guise of observing athletic form—part of my sports medicine studies—but the truth is I'm studying Cassidy.

"Stick the landing, Cass! You got this!" shouts one of the cheerleaders, her voice echoing off the high ceiling. I lean against the bleachers, pretending to jot down notes while really just watching her.

She's Noah's...*situationship.* Does she think they are more? Does she know what he said to me?

Cassidy takes her position at the center of the mats, hazel eyes locked in concentration. She's the epitome of focus—a trait I begrudgingly admire. As the captain calls out the routine, Cassidy launches into motion. It's like she's part of some intricate dance with gravity, each flip and twist defying physics in a way that would have Newton tossing his apple aside in disbelief.

I've seen her nail this routine a dozen times at games, but today there's a hesitation in her jump, a wobble that wasn't there before. My heart stops for a split second, recognizing the precursor to disaster—an injury waiting to happen.

And then it does.

Cassidy lands awkwardly, her ankle folding beneath her in a way that churns my stomach. A collective gasp reverberates around the gym as she crumples to the mat, her face contorted in pain, trying to mask it with that practiced look of indifference.

"Shit," I mutter under my breath, my medical instincts already flaring up despite our complicated history. I know what comes next—the swelling, the bruising, and if she's unlucky, torn ligaments.

"Is she okay?" The concern in the other cheerleaders' voices is palpable as they rush to her side, their pom-poms forgotten mounds of color against the hardwood floor.

"Stay back, give her space!" I hear myself calling out, surprising even me with the urgency in my voice. But I can't help it. Despite everything, seeing Cassidy hurt tugs at something within me—something annoyingly empathetic.

Stepping forward, I prepare to do what I do best—help athletes in trouble—even if the athlete in question is the same girl who's been making my life annoying lately. I'm across the gym floor before my brain catches up with my feet, knees pumping, ponytail swinging. Cassidy's still on the mat, her long dark hair fanned out like a distress signal. I drop to my knees beside her, my hands automatically hovering over her ankle without touching.

"Hey, Cassidy," I say, trying to keep my voice steady and professional. "I'm going to take a look at your calf. Can you tell me where it hurts?"

She tries to sit up, wincing as she attempts to wave me off with a dismissive flick of her wrist. "I'm fine, Lexi. Really, it's just a little twist."

Her voice is tight, though, betraying the pain she must feel. Classic Cassidy Harper—too stubborn to show weakness, even when lying flat on her back in front of the entire cheer squad. It would be almost admirable if it wasn't so exasperating.

"Come on, Cass," I chide gently, not buying it for a second. "You and I both know you're about as 'fine' as I am a synchronized swimmer. Let's not make this worse by being prideful, okay?"

I can see the battle in her—the desire to shrug it off, to maintain that veneer of untouchable cheer captain, versus the reality of her body screaming that something's wrong. She bites her lip and looks away, her shoulders tensing under the strain of maintaining her facade.

"Look, I know we're not exactly besties," I continue, keeping my tone light despite the tension, "but I've seen enough injuries to be in the know. And yours is already starting to swell. Let's treat it now before you need pom-pom festooned crutches just to walk."

For a moment, she seems to consider my words, then she huffs out a breath and nods curtly, finally conceding. It’s a small victory, but I’ll take it. As much as Cassidy and I are rivals, I don't want her hurt—not really. Not when I can do something about it.

"Fine," she relents, her voice softer now, less sure of itself. "But only because you're so annoyingly persistent."

"Persistent is my middle name," I quip, allowing a small smile to play at the corner of my mouth. As I carefully examine her leg from calf to ankle, I ensure I cause as little discomfort as possible. I ease Cassidy's sneaker off with the care of disarming a bomb, her hiss of pain cutting through the gym's charged silence. Her ankle's already puffing up like a marshmallow over an open flame—angry and swollen.

"Okay, Cass," I say, keeping my voice steady, "I need to feel around to see if it's a sprain or something worse. Might be uncomfortable, but I promise, I'm not here to torture you."

She rolls her eyes, wincing as she shifts on the bleachers. "As tempting as that sounds, Lexi, can't we just skip to the part where you magically fix me?"

"Sorry, no magic. Just good old-fashioned medical know-how." My fingers probe gently, testing the tender ligaments. "You'll thank me when you're back cheering and not stuck on the sidelines. Ask Noah—he had a similar sprain."

I wince inside at the mention. If she does have an inkling of his feelings for me, that might have been a bad move.

"Fine," she mutters, gripping the edge of the seat as if bracing for a tidal wave, "just do what you have to do."

"All right, gonna wrap it now," I inform her, reaching for the athletic tape I always keep in my backpack. The tape unspools with a whisper, and with practiced hands, I secure her ankle, the black lines crisscrossing her skin in a pattern only those versed in sports injuries would appreciate.

"Wow, you're pretty good at this," Cassidy admits begrudgingly, watching the tape cocoon her injury.

"Thanks," I reply, trying not to let the compliment from my rival send a weird thrill through me. "Spent more time than I'd like to admit wrapping my own injuries back in high school. Guess it paid off."

"Guess so," she concedes, a shadow of respect flickering in her gaze.

I watch Cassidy's chest rise and fall with a deep breath, her lips parting as if she's about to spill secrets kept locked away for far too long. There's an unguarded look on her face, one I'm not used to seeing on the girl who always seemed untouchable.

"Lexi," she starts, the inflection of my name sounding like the beginning of a confession. "I can't be sidelined now, not when pro scouts could be watching. If I lose my spot because of this..." Her voice trails off, but her gaze is pleading, almost desperate.

"Hey," I say softly, squatting down to her level. "You're not going to lose your spot. You're the best they've got, and everyone knows it."

"It's not just about being the best. It's about staying the best." The vulnerability in her voice catches me off guard. "My parents... they have these expectations. And I've worked so hard, but the pressure, it's like—like I can never do enough, you know?"

"More than you think," I admit. It's true; growing up with a dad who coached hockey, I've felt that same relentless drive to meet expectations, to make him proud. "But sometimes, we put more pressure on ourselves than anyone else does. Your health is important, Cassidy. Without it, you can't meet any expectations, let alone your own."

She looks at me then, really looks at me, and I feel the weight of her scrutiny. "How do you do it? How do you keep pushing forward when everything seems to stack up against you?"

"By remembering why I started in the first place." My hand hovers over her taped ankle. "For the love of the game, right?"

"Right," she echoes, a faint smile tugging at her lips. "Thank you. For...this." She gestures to her ankle and then to her heart, a silent acknowledgment of the support beyond physical injuries.

"Anytime," I assure her, and I mean it. We may be from different worlds, Cassidy Harper and I, but in this moment, there's an understanding between us that goes beyond rivalries. "For what it's worth, I've seen you perform. You're not just coasting on your family's name."

"Thanks." She looks at me, and there's gratitude there, but also something else—something that makes my stomach do a weird little flip. I think of Noah again.

"Look," I continue, my voice steadier than I feel, "I know it's none of my business, but if you ever need to vent about the BS of competitive sports... I'm around."

"Are you offering to be my therapist?" Cassidy teases, though I detect a note of sincerity beneath her jest.

"Let's call it mutual commiseration. A solidarity thing."

"Solidarity," she repeats, testing the weight of the word between us.

"Solidarity," I confirm, with more conviction than I'd expected.

As she nods, there's an unspoken agreement—a truce of sorts—that blossoms in the space between us. And as we stand there in the quiet aftermath, I can't quite shake the feeling that this unexpected connection might just redefine the rules of the game.

If her boyfriend doesn't tell her he's falling for me, that is.

CHAPTER NINETEEN: LEXI

That night, counting down to the big game, I hermit up in my dorm room and wallow in indecision. My graduation cap stares at me from its perch atop a stack of textbooks like it's mocking my indecision. I flop back onto my bed, surrounded by brochures from various physical therapy clinics and sports medicine programs. These were plans for after school—each one whispers promises of a future. But there's another decision I need to make first. And all I can hear is the ticking clock in my head reminding me that time is running out to make a choice.

Stay with The Aces, or go to Chicago.

Wes, who I'm almost committed to, or Noah, who is play-acting at love with someone else, and that someone else isn't as shallow as I first judged her to be?

Chicago means uprooting myself so close to finishing school here, but the resume boost, the bona fides of an internship at the facility—worth it? Ashville is smaller, less prestigious. Coach Thompson is on the overbearing side, and I'm walking on eggshells with him. But staying here means Wes—but also Noah and that complication.

I sit up and run a hand through my hair, pulling it away from my face and into a makeshift ponytail. The air in the room feels heavy with the weight of looming adulthood and the decisions that come with it. It's as if every pamphlet is a diverging path in a dense forest, and I'm supposed to just pick the right one blindfolded.

A sigh escapes me. There's only one man I need right now, and I pick up phone to call him.

***

The evening frost clings to the dead grass as I make my way to the secluded garden on campus. It's a hidden gem that most students overlook, but for me, it's a sanctuary. Nestled between two brick buildings, this patch of nature is where I can breathe, where the weight of impending decisions doesn't feel quite so crushing. Even in winter, it's lovely. I can picture the blooms come spring.

I settle onto the weathered wooden bench, the one with the peeling blue paint that somehow feels like home. I close my eyes and tilt my face up, breathing deep.

"Deep in thought?" The voice, familiar and comforting, pulls me back to reality.

My eyes snap open to find my dad standing there, an affectionate smile crinkling the corners of his eyes. I've never been happier that he lives so close. Lots of twenty-somethings would be thrilled to be on a different continent than their parents. But since mom died—I was in middle school, but it hurts fresh every time I think about it—Dad and I have been inseparable.

"Always," I reply, scooting over. He takes a seat beside me, his presence a solid reassurance.

"Come on, Lexi. Let's grab some hot chocolate. I think we could both use it."

We walk side by side to the cozy café that's become my go-to for late-night study sessions and post-game celebrations. Once we're settled into the squishy armchairs with our steaming drinks, Dad leans forward, his elbows resting on his knees, exuding the same intensity he brought to every game he coached.

"About the internship, Lexi—you've got your mother's spirit but my indecisiveness off the ice," he begins, his gaze steady. "But don't let that stop you from listening to your heart."

I wrap my hands around the ceramic mug, the heat seeping into my palms. "It's not always that simple, Dad."

"Nothing worth having ever is." He chuckles softly, taking a sip of his hot chocolate before continuing. "When I was your age, I thought I had everything figured out. Then life threw me a curveball—your mom."

I can't help but smile at the mention of Mom, her vibrant laughter still echoes in my memories.

"Meeting her changed everything. I had to learn that following my dreams didn't mean giving up on love or family. It meant integrating them into the dream, making it richer."

"But what if my dreams take me one way and... and Wes's go another? Or what if I'm supposed to be with Noah—and that's messy? What if it's neither, but Chicago on my own?" My voice is barely above a whisper, the fear of the answer clawing at my throat.

"Then you talk, you compromise, and sometimes..." He pauses, searching for the right words. "Sometimes, you take a leap of faith. But remember, Lexi, you're a force to be reckoned with—on and off the ice. Don't lose sight of who you are and what you want."

His words settle over me, a gentle reminder of the strength I've always drawn from my family, from the sport that's shaped me. I nod slowly, letting the wisdom of his advice sink in.

"Thanks, Dad. I needed that."

"Anytime, kiddo." He reaches over, squeezing my hand. "Now, finish that hot chocolate before it gets cold. It's not good for the soul to let chocolate go to waste."

"Never," I say with mock solemnity, lifting the mug to my lips. As I drink, the warmth of the chocolate and the warmth of my father's love bolster me, reminding me that no matter where life's rink may take me, I won't be facing it alone.

I check my watch after my mug is empty, and anxiety rears up, fresh. "Dad, I gotta go."

All of my decisions will have to wait—until after playoffs.

CHAPTER TWENTY: LEXI

My heart thumps in sync with the bass-heavy anthem reverberating through the arena. Every cell in my body vibrates with the electric charge of anticipation, as if I'm a live wire, plugged into the collective buzz of the crowd. The air is thick with tension, the kind that heralds in those defining moments that can make or break a season. I lean over the boards, scanning the ice for Noah and Wes, their forms just two amongst the flurry of jerseys.

"Let's go! This is it!" I whisper to myself, though my voice is lost beneath the roar of excitement from the stands. I can't help but feel the adrenaline pumping through my veins, an echo of my days racing across similar ice. The weight of responsibility settles on my shoulders; tonight, I'm not just a spectator, I'm guardian and ally to these athletes.

Suddenly, the puck drops, and like the crack of a starting pistol, everything accelerates. Players surge forward, blades slicing into the ice with precision, a dance of speed and strategy unfolding before me. Noah, with his deft handling, dodges an opposing defenseman, his movements fluid and determined. There's something akin to poetry in the way he skates—like he's writing verses on the ice that only a few can truly read.

I catch sight of Wes, too; his presence on the ice is commanding, magnetic, even. He's a force to be reckoned with, and as he intercepts a pass meant for an opponent, I feel a surge of pride. His focus is laser-sharp, and he maneuvers through the players with the confidence of someone who knows this game isn't just physical—it's mental warfare.

The clang of a puck against the goalpost sends a shiver down my spine, and I jolt forward, gripping the railing. It's a relentless back-and-forth, the players pushing themselves to the brink, every pass and shot a desperate plea for supremacy. It's almost balletic, this chaos, this whirl of color and motion—until it's not.

"Watch the wing!" I find myself shouting, caught up in the moment, as if they could hear me over the cacophony. My professional demeanor wars with the hockey enthusiast inside me, the girl who grew up breathless with each play, each near miss that could have turned the tide.

I barely register the cold seeping through my boots, nor the ache in my clenched fists. All that matters is the game, the exhilarating symphony of sticks and pucks, grunts and shouts, blending into a soundtrack I know by heart. And as each second ticks down, I'm reminded why I'm here, why I've chosen this path of healing and support.

Because this, right here, with the ice beneath their feet and hope coursing through their veins, is where legends are born and dreams are either realized or dashed. And I, Alexis Turner, am part of that. Part of something greater—a story still being written, one shift, one game, one season at a time.

I would miss this in Illinois.

The puck sails past the blue line, and my breath catches as Noah pivots, his skates carving arcs into the ice as he tracks its path. His focus is singular, a captain on his quest, but from the corner of my eye, I see Wes barreling down the opposite wing, a blur of determination and raw power.

"Come on, boys," I mutter under my breath, leaning forward as if I could will them toward victory with my posture alone.

And then it happens—a perfect storm of bad luck and physics. The opposing forward streaks across the ice, his eyes locked onto the puck like a missile seeking its target. But in his path are both Noah and Wes, converging at the same point, unaware of the impending collision.

"Look out!" My voice is lost in the roar of the crowd, a silent plea swallowed by the din.

Their three bodies meet with a sickening crunch, the sound reverberating through the arena and ricocheting around my ribcage. Time slows, the game's rhythm skips a beat, and the crowd falls into a hush laden with dread.

For a moment, I'm frozen, memories of my own childhood injury and the repeat collisions with Noah and Wes flashing behind my eyelids—I feel pain, fear, the hollow echo of dreams shattering. But this isn't about me. This is about Noah and Wes, about their futures hanging in the balance.

My training kicks in, propelling me over the barrier and onto the slick surface of the rink. My heart pounds against my chest, each beat a drumroll as I skate toward them, my ponytail whipping behind me.

"Turner, you wait for Drew!" Thompson yells behind me. I ignore him. Drew's been so scarce lately, shuffling my intern hours off on filler like the cheer practice, that I didn't even look for him when I arrived.

And he’s not coming out—so someone has to.

"Noah! Wes!" I call out, my voice steady despite the adrenaline surging through me.

I reach them, dropping to my knees. Wes's grimacing, his hand hovering near his shoulder, while Noah is trying to push himself up, wincing as he puts weight on his leg.

"Easy," I say, my hands moving with practiced efficiency, gentle but firm. "Let me look."

Around us, players hover like specters, their expressions a mix of concern and frustration—the game paused, their comrades in pain. But my world narrows to the two men before me, their well-being my sole focus.

"Talk to me," I urge, locking eyes first with Noah, then with Wes, looking for signs of clarity, shock, the will to fight.

"Lexi, I'm fine," Wes grunts, his voice rough, but there's a vulnerability there that belies his words.

"Stay still for a second, okay?" I press, my tone leaving no room for argument.

I kneel on the ice, my hands steady despite the chaos around me. Wes's shoulder hangs at an unnatural angle, a clear sign of dislocation, his face contorted as he clutches it close to his chest. The way he winces with every shallow breath tells me this is more than just a simple pop-out; there might be ligament damage.

"Okay, Wes, I need you to focus on breathing for me. Slow and steady," I instruct, flashing back to countless hours spent studying injury protocols. "We're going to immobilize your arm before moving you."

To my side, Noah tries to put weight on his leg and fails, collapsing back onto the ice with a curse. His leg isn't positioned quite right—the bend of his knee suggests a possible meniscus tear or worse, a full ACL injury. Given his history, the latter would be catastrophic, not just for the game but for his season, maybe even his career.

"Hey, Noah, look at me," I say, catching his gaze. It's filled with frustration, that rebellious spark of his dimmed by the reality of injury. "Don't try to stand. We need to brace that leg before we do anything else."

Their injuries are severe, yes, but manageable if treated correctly. This is where my expertise comes in—where my years of study morph into action. As I run through the evaluation protocols in my head, I'm acutely aware of their trust in me. They're my responsibility, and it's up to me to make the call that could define their futures.

"Shoulder's bad," Wes admits through gritted teeth.

"All right, let's take this one step at a time," I say, my mind racing to assess, to plan, to support. I can't let personal feelings cloud my judgment—not when their careers, their passions are at stake.

"Can you breathe okay?" I ask, touching Noah's wrist lightly, gauging his pulse. To Wes, "Any numbness?"

They answer, their voices strong but laced with pain, and I feel a swell of pride amidst the worry. These are athletes—my athletes—and I'll be damned if I don't do everything in my power to protect them.

"Let's get you off the ice and properly checked out," I decide, looking back to see that Drew is skating out toward us. And he has medics with him. Good. Maybe Drew was in the stands—sometimes, the bravest thing an athlete can do is acknowledge when they're hurt, and the smartest thing a physical therapist can do is listen—to their bodies, to their hearts, to the subtle cues that whisper the difference between a quick recovery and a lasting damage.

"Stick with me, guys," I say, offering a smile that's equal parts reassurance and challenge. "We're going to get through this together."

It's not just their physical well-being hanging in the balance; it's the team's morale, their shot at victory, and possibly the trajectory of their careers. But right now, all I can think about is ensuring they receive the care they need. Because that's what I do—I heal, I support, I fight for my athletes' chance to play another day. And I'll be damned if I let them down now.

With the medics flanking either side, my eyes dart between Noah's grimace and Wes's clenched jaw. The crowd's anxious murmurs fade into the background as Coach Thompson jogs onto the ice.

"Coach," I say. "Both injuries are severe. Wes's got a dislocated shoulder, Noah might have a torn ligament. We need to rule out fractures."

"Lexi, what are you saying? Can they play?" Coach's voice is urgent, almost desperate.

"I doubt it."

Thompson grimaces. He turns to Drew. "I want a real medical opinion," he snaps.

Drew shoots Thompson a look. "Let her work." He is brisk but not unkind; there's no room for softness when careers are on the line.

Thompson nods grudgingly and steps back.

"What do you think?" Drew's asking me—relying on my opinion.

My fingers probe gently around Wes's shoulder, feeling the abnormality beneath his pads. He tries to mask the pain, but his sharp intake of breath gives it away.

“Where were you?” I ask Drew as I work.

His eyes darken. “Thompson asked me to start the ice baths for after the game. Maybe he’s psychic.”

Maybe he wanted you out of the way, I think.

Wes cries out as I press at the area around his shoulder.

"Easy, Wes. You're in good hands," I reassure him, trying to convey confidence I'm not entirely sure I feel. His nod tells me he hears more than my words, he feels the promise behind them.

"Stabilize first, assess after," I instruct the nearby EMT, who nods and gets to work on Noah's leg. The bond between an athlete and their physical therapist is sacred, built on moments like this—of vulnerability, trust, and the silent understanding that we're in this fight together.

"Lexi," Wes starts, his voice strained. "I can't feel..."

"Hey, hey," I cut him off gently, my hand finding his. "Focus on my voice, okay? You're going to be all right. We'll take it one step at a time."

"Will I..." He doesn't finish, but he doesn't have to. The fear in his eyes speaks volumes.

"Let's not get ahead of ourselves." The coach's demands echo in my head, but right now, it's just Wes and me on the ice. "You're strong, Wes. Stronger than anyone I know."

Wes’s grip tightens minutely around my hand—a silent a lifeline in the eye of uncertainty. And in that moment, the world narrows down to the task at hand, to the trust placed squarely on my shoulders. The cold bites at my cheeks as I kneel on the ice, my senses numb to everything but the task before me. I'm a fortress of calm amidst the chaos, even as my heart thunders against my ribs.

"Lexi," Wes’s voice is strained, his usually steady tone laced with pain. "I can still play. Just pop it back in, tape it up, and I'm good to go."

"Easy, Jacobs." My words are gentle, almost motherly. "I know you'd skate through a hurricane for this team, but we've got to think long-term here."

"Long-term is now," he insists, the words accompanied by a wince as he tries to move. "We need this win, Lexi. The team needs me. My scholarship…my mom…"

A groan from my other side pulls my attention. Noah is lying flat, his leg stretched out awkwardly. Unlike Wes, he doesn't try to mask his discomfort; instead, he lets it show in the hard set of his jaw, the furrow between his brows deepening.

"Dammit, Turner, you've seen me skate with worse. Just give me something for the pain and let me back out there," Wes growls, frustration seeping into his voice like a storm cloud threatening to burst.

"Even if I did, Wes, your arm might not agree with your hero complex," I reply, trying to keep the mood light despite the gravity of the situation. "That could turn a short recovery into a season-ender."

"Season-ender?" His voice cracks like thin ice, the façade of the untouchable bad boy melting away to reveal the raw fear beneath. "No, screw that. I'm not leaving my team hanging."

I look between the two of them, each so different yet united in their resolve. The weight of their trust sits heavy on my shoulders. They're not just athletes under my care; they're people I've come to respect... and more.

"Lexi, we need a decision," Thompson presses, hovering over us.

"Give me a minute!" I snap, then immediately soften my tone for Wes and Noah. "Guys, listen to me. I'm going to do everything in my power to get you both back out here when you're ready. But I won't risk your health for one game."

Their eyes meet mine, and there's an unspoken agreement in that shared glance. They trust me to make the call, even if it's the last thing any of us want. Their nods are reluctant, their expressions a mix of resignation and unyielded spirit.

“I agree,” Drew says. “They’re out.”

Before Thompson can protest further, Drew blows the whistle around his neck and signals off-ice. A stretcher for both Wes and Noah are wheeled out, a spectacle that Thompson doesn’t have time to stop.

"All right, let's move them," I signal to the medics, and as the stretchers glide across the ice, carrying away more than just two injured players, I feel the weight of impending decisions heavy on my chest. But that weight doesn't bow me. It galvanizes me—because I am Lexi Turner, healer of warriors, guardian of dreams, and no matter what comes next, I stand ready.

"Trust me, guys," I assure them, my confidence bolstered by their faith in me. "I won't let you down."

"Never thought you would," Noah says, his eyes softening with a gratitude that does funny things to my heart—no matter how much I try to keep this professional. His voice is slurred with pain, and as he is lifted away, he calls back, “Think about what I said the other night—Lexi, this is real.”

Then, he promptly passes out.

I suddenly feel Wes’s gaze on me, intense. A stretcher is lowered onto the ice next to him.

“What is he talking about, Lex?”

I avert my gaze, pretending to be engrossed with the medical supplies in my bag. "It's nothing," I mutter, my palms sweating against the cool handles of the bag.

Wes grabs my wrist, forcing me to look at him, his startling blue eyes now tinged with concern...or is it something more? Is there pain that has nothing to do with his shoulder? "That didn't sound like nothing."

I try to pull my hand away, but he doesn't let go. His grip is firm yet gentle. "It's between Noah and me," I say, fighting the urge to reveal too much.

With a sigh, he releases my hand. His expression is unreadable, a thoughtful furrow in his brow as he acknowledges my words with a curt nod. Yet, something in his gaze is less fiery, more reserved. "Okay then."

I can't tell if it's pain or disappointment I see. To mask my own discomfort, I start fussing about with his gear again. “I'll see you in the hospital later," I say, trying to keep my voice steady. “Do you want me to call your mom?”

He looks at me, surprised. "No need for that," he says quickly, the words rushing out like a reflex. His gaze averts down to the ice, focusing on anything but me. He's quiet for a moment, his jawline tight, before he finally speaks. "And as far as coming to the hospital—don't bother, Lex."

His words cut through me like a winter chill, and I'm left standing there, my breath visible in the cold rink air as the medics start to wheel him away. I can't help but watch as he's taken off ice, his tall figure receding in the distance until I'm left alone on the frozen expanse. There's an indescribable silence that follows—the quiet before the storm—and I feel it reverberating in my chest. Suddenly, the weight of everything just got a little heavier. It's clear there's more at stake now, and it's not just about hockey anymore.

I follow the trail they've left on the ice as I let Wes's words sink in. *Don't bother, Lex.* The finality in his voice echoes hauntingly in my mind. Stinging, like the bitter cold that seeps through my layers and resonates along every nerve ending, making me realize that nothing will ever be the same again.

Everyone is looking at me. Coach Turner, the assistant coaches, the spectators, Drew—and my face flames. In the sudden void his departure leave, I know there are no winners tonight—only broken hearts and bruised egos.

"Turner, off the ice," Thompson barks—but it's softer than his usual tone.

As the players resume their positions and the puck drops, I can only watch, hoping that my next choice won't be the one that shatters hearts. With bated breath, I wait for the next collision, the next shot, the next scream from the crowd that might signal triumph or disaster.

And as the game plays out in front of me, I realize that no matter the outcome, nothing will ever be the same again. Not for Noah, not for Wes, and certainly not for me.

CHAPTER TWENTY ONE: LEXI

The hospital's sterile scent wraps around me like an unwelcome embrace as I push through the automatic doors. My heart's doing that uncomfortable flutter-tap dance again, heavy with a cocktail of anticipation and nerves. It's Noah and Wes on my mind—Noah with his warm, understanding eyes, and Wes, all brooding intensity wrapped in a blanket of smoldering glances.

I'm here for Noah first, ready to clear the air, but it's the upcoming face-off with Wes that has my stomach twisting into Gordian knots. Noah dropped the bomb; he's got feelings for me, feelings that go way beyond our easy friendship. And now? Now, I'm about to see him, hoping to God I can navigate through this without tripping over my own feet.

I shuffle down the hallway, my sneakers squeaking against the polished linoleum floor, each step bringing me closer to what feels like a defining moment. Nurses pass by in colorful scrubs, offering sympathetic smiles or buried in their charts, and somewhere a baby cries out—a reminder that life, in all its messy glory, doesn't stop for heartache or confusion.

Room 318 is lit by the soft glow of morning sun filtering through the blinds, casting lines across Noah's bed where he lays propped up by pillows, a cast rendering one leg immobile. I waited until this morning to come—it took me that long to work up the nerve. Noah's smile is a proof of his undying optimism, even though he's marooned here, sidelined by injury.

"Hey," I say, forcing brightness into my voice as I edge closer to the foot of his bed, careful not to disturb the tangle of tubes and wires. "How's the captain doing today?"

"Lexi!" He perks up, and it's almost as if we're back at the rink, strategizing plays, except the roles have shifted, and I'm not sure of mine anymore. "I've been waiting for you. Feeling better than last night. You know, one day closer to getting back out there."

He's all determination and heart—qualities that made me admire him long before I knew him as anything more than the guy steering his team toward victory. The kind of guy who could make a girl forget herself, her own compass spinning wildly out of true north.

"Good to hear," I reply, mustering a smile while my insides churn with words I'm not ready to say. Not yet. First, I need to square things with Noah, set the record straight. We've always been honest with each other, and I won't let that change—not even for the sake of sparing feelings or avoiding the hard truths. But damn, this is going to be as pleasant as a puck to the face.

"Lexi." His smile is warm, but there's a tension in his face that suggests he knows this isn't a regular visit. "What's up?"

I take a deep breath, the air feeling heavier than I remember from a moment ago. "We need to talk."

"Sounds serious." He tries to make light of it, but his smile doesn't quite reach his eyes anymore.

"It is." I pull up a chair beside him, my hands fidgeting in my lap. "Noah, you know I care about you, right? As a friend, I mean."

"Of course," he says, his voice steady. His bruised hand finds mine, giving it a reassuring squeeze that I wish I could fully return.

"And because I care about you, I have to be honest. You're with Cassidy, and we both know that neither of us is the type to hurt people intentionally."

He nods slowly, a shadow passing over his expression. "Yeah, I know."

"Your feelings... they caught me off guard, and I got swept up in them," I confess, my throat tightening. "But it wasn't fair, not to you, not to Cassidy, and definitely not to me. Because... my heart, it's somewhere else, Noah."

The words spill out in a rush, like a puck sliding across ice—too fast to stop once they've started. Noah releases my hand, folding his arms across his chest as he leans back, processing.

"Is it Wes?" There's no accusation in his tone, just the calm clarity I've always admired.

"Does it matter?" I hedge, uncomfortable with the way he stares at me, unflinching.

"Yeah, it does. Because if it's Wes..." He pauses, a soft chuckle escaping him despite the gravity of our conversation. "Then I know you're in good hands. He's a decent guy, despite what happens on the ice."

"Decent" feels like an understatement when it comes to describing Wes, but now is not the time for that conversation. "We're still friends, right?" I ask instead, desperate for some semblance of normalcy between us.

"Always, Lex," he assures me, reaching for my hand again, his grip gentle yet firm. "You're too good at taping up my injuries for me to let you go."

I can't help but laugh, the sound mingling with relief and lingering sadness. "I'll hold you to that, Captain."

There's also *that* secret I'm still keeping. The internship.

"Good," he says, his easy smile returning. "Because I'm going to need you more than ever when I'm back on the ice."

"Deal," I reply, knowing full well that my role might change, but our friendship is one constant in a game that never stops shifting beneath our skates. I squeeze Noah's hand, the steady beat of his pulse grounding me. The fluorescent lights hum above us, and the antiseptic scent of the hospital fills my senses as I brace for what comes next.

"Lex," Noah says, his voice carrying a warmth that belies the sterile environment, "I want you to know that I'm genuinely happy for you and Wes. Seriously. If there's anyone who can handle your verbal slapshots, it's him."

A laugh bubbles up from my chest, the tension easing from my shoulders. It's just like Noah to break the ice with a joke. "You think my slapshots are that bad?"

"Only when you aim them at me." He grins, then grows serious again. "But really, Lexi, I mean it. You two... you've got something special. And if he makes you happy, that's all that matters to me."

"Thanks, Noah." The words come out more choked than I intend. His support means everything, especially now when everything feels so tenuous.

He shifts in the hospital bed, grimacing slightly before settling back against the pillows. "I need to tell you something, too. Something important."

"Anything," I say, ready to listen.

Noah takes a deep breath, his gaze drifting to the window where snowflakes dance against the glass like miniature ice skaters. "It's about the farm—my family's farm. Things haven't been going well. They're... failing, actually. My folks want me to come home, help figure things out."

My heart clenches. Noah's family farm is more than just land and crops; it's a legacy, a piece of him. "I'm so sorry, Noah."

He continues, the words spilling out like water from a broken dam. "And with this injury..." He glances down at his bandaged ankle. "The doctors are talking serious rehab, surgery to get things right. Hockey's off the table for a while. Maybe for good."

"Hey, don't talk like that." Instinctively, I reach out, smoothing the crease between his brows. "You're the strongest person I know. You'll get through this."

"Strong or not," he says, locking eyes with me, "it's a lot to take in, you know? But having friends like you—it makes the tough stuff a little less heavy."

"Always here for you, Captain," I reaffirm, squeezing his hand once more. There's a resilience in Noah that can weather any storm, and I believe in him, even if the path ahead looks like an uncharted stretch of ice.

"Thanks, Lex," he says, a smile cracking through the worry on his face. "That means a lot."

We sit in silence for a moment, both lost in our thoughts. Snow continues to fall outside, cloaking the world in a soft white blanket. Inside, we find comfort in the familiarity of friendship, knowing that some bonds can withstand any hit.

I stand up, my chair scraping lightly against the sterile hospital floor. The sound echoes too loudly in the quiet room, a sharp reminder of reality cutting through our bubble of camaraderie. Noah watches me, his eyes a mix of pain and determination that I've come to know well on the ice. It's strange to see that same look here, in a hospital room, but it's Noah. He's always been a fighter.

"Listen, Noah," I start, my voice steady even though my heart isn't. "You can't let this... any of this beat you. You're not just a hockey player; you're a brilliant strategist on the ice. That brain of yours?" I tap my temple with a smirk. "It's your best asset."

He chuckles, the tension easing from his shoulders at my words. "Thanks, Lexi, but strategy doesn't fix torn ligaments or pay the bills."

"Maybe not directly, but there are other ways to stay in the game. Coaching, commentating, hell, even sports psychology. You've got options." I'm brainstorming aloud now, each idea a buoy to keep him afloat. "You could be great at any of them."

"Easy for you to say, Miss Future-PT-for-the-stars," he teases, but I can tell he's mulling it over.

"Seriously, Noah. We'll figure something out. And I'm not just saying that because we're friends." I pause, my resolve hardening. "I'm saying it because I know what it's like to have the game ripped away before you're ready. I won't sit back and watch it happen to you too."

"Lex—" he starts, but I hold up a hand.

"Let me help. Maybe there's a way to combine rehab and study. Get ahead on your coaching certs while you recover. Use that big brain for something other than memorizing stats for on-ice antics."

"Okay, okay," he concedes, a slow grin spreading across his face. "Sounds like you won't take no for an answer. So, when do we start?"

"I—you tell me," I declare, and then softer, "We'll tackle it together, one step at a time."

Even if we have to do it long-distance.

"Deal." Noah nods, and I can feel the shift in the room—the weight of despair lifting, replaced by a tentative hope.

"Good. Now rest up, because you're going to need all the energy you can get." I waggle my eyebrows playfully, earning another laugh from him.

"Will do, Doctor Turner." His use of my future title sends a warm surge of pride through me.

"Get some sleep, Captain." I pull my coat tighter around me, preparing to leave.

"Bye, Lex." His voice follows me out, carrying a note of gratitude that wraps around me like a blanket.

I need air before I go see Wes.

Outside, the snow is still falling, blanketing everything in hushed white. It's beautiful, serene—nature's way of reminding us that after every storm, there's a fresh start waiting. As I walk through the quiet hospital corridors, the click of my boots on the tile floor syncs with the rhythm of new possibilities. For Noah, hopefully for Wes, and for me.

The cold air hits me as I step outside, and I tilt my head back to catch snowflakes on my tongue. They melt instantly, a fleeting sensation that's as sweet as it is ephemeral. Just like this moment of peace in the chaos of life. I shove my hands into my coat pockets and exhale a cloud of foggy breath. The promise I made to Noah lingers in my mind, echoing with every crunch of snow under my boots. I can't shake off the intensity of our exchange, the way his vulnerability cracked open something inside me.

I pause at the edge of the hospital's parking lot, letting the moment sink in. This is where everything changes, isn't it? It's not just about hearts and hand-holding; it's about futures and dreams and picking up pieces when life checks you hard against the boards. I need to be strong—not just for myself, but for the guys who have become more than just teammates. They're my tribe. My people.

I replay Noah's confession, how he laid bare his fears about the farm and his future. I think about what it means to stand by someone when they're facing the kind of uncertainty that can make your soul feel like it's trapped in a penalty box. There's no playbook for this. No coach shouting strategies from the sidelines.

But I turn back to the hospital, knowing—it’s time to make my final play.

CHAPTER TWENTY TWO: LEXI

I'm rounding the corner, my sneakers squeak against the polished floor of the hospital hallway. My heart is a frantic drummer in my chest, not from the run here but from what awaits me behind Wes's room door. I shake out my hands, trying to dispel the nervous energy crackling through my veins when a shadow looms over me.

"Turner."

The deep voice is as unwelcome as an ice bath, and I freeze mid-step. Coach Thompson stands there, his broad shoulders blocking the path ahead like a goalie defending his net. His eyes are flinty, his jaw set in that familiar stubborn line that spells trouble.

"Coach Thompson," I say, forcing my tone to stay even despite the surge of annoyance. "I was just—"

"Save it." He cuts me off with a dismissive wave of his hand. "You stepped way out of bounds today, Turner. Pulling Wes and Noah out of the game? That's not your call. I don't care what Drew says."

My fingers twitch, itching for the comfort of the notebook tucked inside my bag—the one filled with evidence of every shortcut and wrong turn he has steered this team toward. But I hold my ground, meeting his glare head-on. "They were hurt, Coach. Seriously hurt. Playing them could've made it worse."

"An intern doesn't make those calls." His voice is a low growl now, a clear warning. "You've got a lot of nerve, Lexi. You want to make it in this field, you can't let sentimentality get in the way of the game."

"Integrity is more important than any game," I retort, my own temper flaring despite the risks.

"Is it worth your internship?" There's a steel edge to his question. "Because keep pushing like this, and I'll have no choice but to let you go. This is your future, Lexi. Think about it."

I clench my jaw, tasting the bitter tang of frustration. The threat hangs between us, heavy as a puck before a penalty shot. But I don't waver. Not when it comes to the safety of the players. Not even if it means facing off against Coach Thompson.

"Is that all, Coach?" I ask, my voice steady despite the inner turmoil.

He studies me for a long, silent moment, then steps aside. "For now."

As I pass him, the tension in my shoulders eases, but not by much. I'm playing a dangerous game, but it's one I have to see through to the end—for Wes, for Noah, for every athlete who's been pushed too far. I square my shoulders, the weight of my notebook a solid reassurance against my side. "Actually, Coach," I interject before he can fully pivot away, "there's something you should know."

Coach Thompson's eyes narrow, his posture rigid like a ref about to call a penalty. "What's that?"

"Section 4, Article 3, Subsection B." The numbers roll off my tongue as I tap my notebook through my bag, picturing the dates neatly written, the paper's edges frayed from constant use. "It explicitly states that a player with a suspected concussion must be removed from play immediately. Remember when you made that rookie stay in after the headshot? But let's not stop there. How about we discuss the entire season? Because I've got every single violation documented in here." I pat my notebook for emphasis. "Including all the times you pushed Wes and Noah to keep on the ice for these exact same injuries."

"Thompson's Rulebook, I call it. Think it's different than what the league says is safe and regulatory?" There's nothing humorous about putting athletes at risk. And while I'm usually all about the banter, right now, I'm shooting straighter than Wes on a breakaway.

"Lexi..." His voice is a warning, but I cut through it.

"Imagine the Dean flipping through these pages. It's a story of ambition over ethics, isn't it?" I tilt my head, feigning contemplation. "Or maybe it's more of a tragedy. Star coach loses everything because he wanted to win—no matter the cost."

The color drains from his face. This is no longer a game of cat-and-mouse; it's checkmate, and he knows it.

"All right." The word is clipped, punctuated with defeat. He steps back, his authority deflated like a puck slashed out of the air. "We're done here."

"Good choice," I say, but as he retreats down the hallway, I can't help a parting shot. "And just so we're clear, my future will never be worth more than someone's health. You might want to remember that."

I watch him go, his shoulders slumped—a stark contrast to the bullish coach who always seemed larger than life. It's a small victory, sure, but it's one for the team. For Wes. For Noah.

Taking a deep breath, I turn toward Wes's room again, my heart pounding a nervous rhythm. Time to face another battle, but this one, I hope, ends with a different kind of win.

I stride down the hallway, a buoyant swagger in my step. My pulse still sings with adrenaline, but it's a harmonious tune now, not the frantic staccato of confrontation. I can't help the smile that dances on my lips; I've done something good today—no, something great.

"Lexi!" The higher, feminine voice slicing through the corridor catches me off guard, and I halt, turning to see Cassidy Harper jogging lightly toward me.

"Hey," I say, guarding my expression. Despite everything, Cassidy and I are more rivals than friends. But the concern etched into her features softens my stance.

"I saw what happened back there with Coach Thompson." Her voice is warm, genuine, and I'm reminded that beneath the privilege and polished exterior lies someone who loves the game as much as I do.

"Thanks," I reply, tucking a loose strand of hair behind my ear. "It was time someone took him on."

"More than time," she agrees, and there's an edge of respect in the words that wasn't there before. "And hey, thanks again for helping me out with my ankle the other day. You didn't have to do that."

"Of course, I did," I respond automatically. "You needed help. We're a team, aren't we?" The words feel foreign yet fitting, like a borrowed jersey that somehow fits just right.

"Guess we are," Cassidy says, and there's a tentative smile on her face that mirrors my own. For a moment, we simply stand there, two people who've seen each other at their worst, finding common ground in a shared purpose.

"Look, about all that animosity between us—" I begin, but she waves me off.

"Water under the bridge," she says, and there's a playful glint in her eye. "Who knows, maybe next time you'll be the one needing saving from a wild puck."

"Or maybe next time we'll both be saving the team from another one of Thompson's crazy plays," I quip back, and we share a laugh, light and unburdened.

"Maybe," she nods, the beginnings of a friendship budding in the space between us.

We walk together—though I'm avoiding going into Wes's. No way do I want her there for that. As we reach the junction leading to Noah's room, she pauses, and I can't help but notice the way her fingers twist nervously around the strap of her purse.

"Actually, Lexi," Cassidy says, her voice taking on a softer quality that seems out of place with the brisk confidence she usually exudes, "I'm here to see Noah."

Oh. Of course. The pieces click into place—the concern etched in her features, the careful make-up that can't quite hide the worry lines. It dawns on me then; this isn't about rivalry or one-upmanship. Cassidy is genuinely worried about Noah, and the realization is oddly disarming.

"Hey, that's really sweet of you," I find myself saying, and I mean it. "Noah's a great guy. He deserves someone looking out for him."

She looks up at me, hazel eyes wide with a vulnerability I've never seen from her before. "You think so?"

"Absolutely." I nod, encouragingly. "I know he'll appreciate it. Noah's had a rough time with the injury... and with everything else." I don't have to elaborate; we both understand the weight 'everything else' carries.

Cassidy takes a deep breath, bolstered by my words, and her usual poise slips back into place like armor. "Thanks, Lexi. That means a lot, coming from you."

"Take good care of him, okay?" The words are simple, but they're a promise, an acknowledgment of the shift between us. From rivals to something resembling friends, united by a common concern for the people around us.

"Will do." Cassidy's smile is genuine as she turns and heads towards Noah's room, her determination clear in the purposeful tilt of her chin. Watching her go, I feel an unexpected kinship with her. Maybe there's more to Cassidy Harper than meets the eye.

I watch Cassidy's retreating figure, a blend of gratitude and newfound respect blossoming between us. Her heels click rhythmically against the tiled floor, each step echoing the tentative bridge we've constructed over the chasm that was once our rivalry. With a final glance over her shoulder, she disappears around the corner.

"Good luck," I whisper to the empty corridor, my words meant for both Cassidy and Noah. Then, I pivot on my heel, squaring my shoulders as I face the closed door at the end of the hallway. Behind it waits Wes, and with him, a conversation I've been both dreading and craving.

My heart thrums a staccato rhythm against my ribs, threatening to break free from its bony cage. I'm not just nervous; I'm a rookie player stepping onto the ice for a championship game. I stop outside his door, pressing my hand to my chest in an attempt to calm the fluttering inside. It's ridiculous, this reaction. I'm Lexi Turner, the girl who doesn't get flustered, especially not by guys like Wes Jacobs—no matter how the sight of him gliding across the ice ignites something wild within me.

A deep breath fills my lungs, and I push the door open.

CHAPTER TWENTY THREE: LEXI

I push open the door to Wes's hospital room, my heart hammering against my ribcage. The sterile scent of antiseptic fills my nostrils here, too, as I step inside, trying to weave a mask of confidence into my features. Wes lies propped up in the bed, his shoulder bandaged and immobilized, but it's the iciness in his ice-blue eyes that sends a chill down my spine.

"Hey," I begin, my voice echoing slightly in the too-quiet room. "How are you feeling?"

He shifts, his jaw tightening. "What does it look like, Turner?" His tone is as cold as the compress probably tucked beneath his sling.

"Like you've seen better days," I quip, forcing a tight smile, not letting him see he's gotten under my skin. The guy could cut glass with his mood right now.

"Thanks for the observation." He looks away, staring out the window at the gray sky beyond. "But I told you not to bother coming."

I pull up the visitor's chair and sit down, crossing my legs. Ignoring the sting of his dismissal, I dive headfirst into safer waters. "So, the Aces pulled through without their star forward and their captain." I watch his face for a reaction. "We won the game."

"Great," he says flatly, not meeting my gaze. "Party on without me then."

I let out a laugh that doesn't quite sound genuine. "Oh, come on, Jacobs. You know it's not the same without you stirring up trouble on the ice. And Noah being all... captain-y."

The corner of his mouth twitches, and I know I've scored a tiny point. "Captain-y, huh? Is that a technical term, Sports Medicine Major?"

"Very technical. Only the most elite understand it." I lean back, a playful challenge in my voice. "You'd have been proud, though. Hartley actually passed the puck for once. Voluntarily."

"Miracles never cease," he mutters, but there's a glimmer of warmth creeping into his voice.

"Exactly. Maybe he finally realized hockey is a team sport. Or maybe... it was just because you weren't there to hog the puck." I raise an eyebrow, inviting him to banter back with me.

"Ha. Funny." Wes finally cracks a small grin, and the tension in the room eases just a fraction. "Just for that, when I'm back on the ice, I'll score a goal exclusively for you. No hogging involved."

"Promise?" I ask, holding his gaze.

"Promise." And there it is, the faintest spark of the Wes Jacobs I know, the one who can charm his way out of (or into) anything. But as our eyes lock, there's something else there, too—something that feels dangerously like hope fluttering in my chest.

"Promise" hangs between us like a puck suspended mid-air, moments before a critical shot. Wes shifts slightly on the hospital bed, wincing with the movement, but his blue eyes are steady on mine. Maybe it's the softened look in them or the way the harsh hospital light seems less sterile suddenly, but I feel the room's chill starting to thaw.

"Mom's coming to stay," he says out of nowhere, and it takes me a second to switch gears.

"Your mom?" The surprise must be evident in my voice because he nods, a trace of vulnerability flickering across his usually stoic face.

"Yep. She's moving here temporarily. We're getting an apartment together." His fingers fiddle with the edge of the thin hospital blanket. "She doesn't want me leaving school, but she can do chemo here. It'll help me be less anxious, her all alone. Gonna take care of each other, I guess."

My heart squeezes tight, sympathy mingling with admiration. "That's... really brave, Wes." I mean every word. It's not just about hockey with him, despite his tough exterior.

"Brave or stupid," he mutters, trying to smile, but there's no real humor in it. "I'm going to be a guy living with his mom."

"Brave," I affirm. "Definitely brave."

There's a comfort in the silence that follows, a shared understanding that some battles are fought off the ice, too. I rack my brain, trying to come up with something to say that won't sound hollow or insincere—or spark another fight—when my thoughts drift to Noah and his own quiet strength in the face of adversity.

"Speaking of brave," I start, hesitating for a fraction of a second, "I think you deserve to know what Noah was talking about on the rink. He, um, he told me he had feelings for me." My words hang heavy, laden with implications and unspoken feelings.

Wes's expression doesn't change immediately, but I see the flicker of something—pain? resignation?—in his face before he schools his features into practiced indifference. "Did he now?"

I nod, biting my lip. "I went to see him earlier, just before I came here." Guilt gnaws at me; I'm not even sure why I'm confessing this to Wes. Maybe because I need him to understand that my heart isn't swayed by grand gestures or confessions made in vulnerable moments. It's won in small doses, in the little things that add up to the big realizations.

"Sounds like a soap opera episode," Wes quips, but the sharpness is gone from his tone. He's trying, I can tell. Trying to be the friend, the teammate who handles things with grace, even when they hurt.

"More like a bad romcom," I retort, trying to keep the mood light, even as my pulse races with the weight of my own confession hovering on the tip of my tongue. But it stays there, unspoken for now, as we both pretend that this conversation is just another play in our ongoing game of verbal hockey.

I shift awkwardly in the sterile hospital chair, the plastic creaking under the tension. Wes stares out the window, his profile etched against the waning light of the day. His jaw clenches as he turns back to me, the ice-blue intensity of his gaze locking onto mine.

"Look, Lexi," he starts, voice measured but distant, "if you've got feelings for Noah, I get it. He's a great guy—captain material. You have my blessing or whatever."

The words sting more than I expect, and I'm momentarily frozen, my mind scrambling to redirect this conversation that's veering off course. "Wes, no," I interject quickly, "you've got it all wrong."

Wes studies me, his expression unreadable. Then, with a sigh, he turns his gaze toward the window, where the orange hues of sunset spill across the sky. "I guess I always figured you and Noah would end up together. You're both so... good." There's a hint of bitterness in his voice, and it stings more than I expect.

"Good?" I scoff, crossing my arms. "You make it sound like we're a pair of golden retrievers."

"Lexi, c'mon. You know what I mean." He shifts uncomfortably in the hospital bed, wincing as he moves his shoulder. "You're the kind of girl who deserves someone who can give her everything. Not a guy who spends as much time in the penalty box as he does on the ice."

"Is that what you think this is about?" I throw my hands up, exasperated. "Matching stat sheets? Because if it is, then you've got me all wrong, Wes. I don't care about 'good' or 'bad,' I care about real. And whatever this is between us—it's the realest thing I've felt in a long time."

"Lexi..." His voice trails off, and for a moment, there's a vulnerability there that I've never seen before. He raises a brow, skepticism still written all over his face, and I realize it's now or never. I need to lay it all out on the line, just like I'd coach one of the Aces through a game-changing play.

"Listen," I say with more conviction, leaning forward so that there's no space for misunderstandings between us, "I care about Noah, yeah, but not like that. The person I want... it's you, Wes. Always has been."

A flicker of surprise crosses his features, and I rush on before he can interject. "And I've decided on Chicago—or, rather, against it. I'm not going anywhere. My plans are right here in Ashville with the Aces. I want to be part of what we're building, on and off the ice. I want to show what I can do, not just for others, but for us—for you and your mom. I'm going to help Noah, too. His ankle isn't going to be the easy road your shoulder will be. He's going to need help down an alternate path."

For a moment, the room is silent except for the faint beeping of the monitor beside his bed. I watch as something shifts in Wes, the walls he's built around himself wavering in the wake of my confession.

"Lexi..." His voice trails off, and there's a vulnerability there that I've only seen glimpses of before. It's raw and real, and it makes my heart ache to see him this way—yet it also fills me with hope.

"Your mom won't be alone in this, and neither will you," I say softly, reaching out to gently grasp his hand, mindful of his injured shoulder. "I'm staying. After the playoffs, for your recovery, for whatever comes next. We're a team, Wes. And I'm playing for keeps."

I inch closer to the edge of Wes's hospital bed, where he lies cocooned in a tangle of white sheets and that slightly sweet sterile scent of antiseptic. The room is dim, save for the slant of sunlight that dares to trespass through the blinds, casting long shadows across his face.

"Look, I know you've got your hands full with... well, everything." My voice echoes slightly in the quiet room. "But your mom doesn't have to go through chemo alone, and neither do you. I've learned a thing or two about physical therapy, you know?" A tentative smile plays at the corners of my lips. "I could help her with some exercises, make sure she's keeping up her strength, but not overdoing it. And you," I pause, gauging his reaction, "you're going to need someone to keep that stubborn shoulder in check."

His gaze softens, thawing into something like gratitude—or is it something more? It's hard to tell with Wes, but I feel like I'm on the right track.

"Lexi, I—" He tries again, the rough timbre of his voice betraying a tremor of emotion. I watch as he swallows hard, as if the words are caught somewhere in his throat.

"Hey, it's okay," I interject quickly, not wanting him to strain himself. "You don't have to say anything. Just think about it, all right?"

But Wes shakes his head, eyes locked onto mine, and I realize he's not struggling with the offer, but rather with something much weightier.

"Lexi, *I* need to tell *you* something," he says, and there's an urgency there that pins me in place. "I've been an idiot about a lot of things, but one thing I know—"

He pauses, draws in a deep breath, and when he speaks again, his voice is laced with a raw honesty that makes my heart skip a beat.

"I love you, Lexi."

The words hang in the air between us, charged and potent, and for a moment, I forget how to breathe. The world narrows down to this room, to Wes, to the truth that resonates in his confession.

"God, Wes," I exhale, a laugh bubbling up from somewhere deep within me, borne out of relief, joy, and a love that's been simmering just beneath the surface for longer than I care to admit. "You have no idea how long I've wanted to hear you say that."

I bridge the gap between us, my heart pounding out a rhythm that's as reckless as it is hopeful. Wes watches me, vulnerable. My hands are surprisingly steady as I cup his face, and with a courage I never knew I had, I lean in.

Our lips meet, and it's a collision of every unsaid word, every stolen glance we've ever shared. His mouth is warm and insistent against mine, and for a moment, there's no injury, no pain—just Wes and me and the kind of kiss that writes its own rules.

"Ouch!" Wes hisses suddenly, pulling back with a wince.

"Oh my God! Your shoulder!" Panic floods through me as I spring back, hands flying to my mouth. "I'm so sorry, I forgot!"

He grunts, rubbing at his shoulder with a pained smile. "It's okay," he says, though his voice is strained. "Worth it."

I hover, unsure whether to laugh or launch into an apology spree. But then, his hand finds mine, and he tugs me gently back toward him. This time when our lips touch, it's a softer connection, more careful but no less charged.

We're both grinning as we adjust to accommodate his injury, finding a new rhythm that's uniquely ours. And as we kiss again, this perfect imperfection of a moment, I can't help but think that happiness doesn't always come neatly packaged—it sometimes arrives with a bump to a dislocated shoulder and in the middle of a hospital room.

I pull back, biting my lip as Wes's ice-blue eyes search mine, looking for something I'm not sure I can put into words.

"Lexi," he says softly, breaking through my whirlwind of thoughts. "What are we doing?"

His question hangs in the air, thick and heavy. I know what he's really asking: Are we a real thing? Can two people who started on opposite sides of an invisible line truly find common ground?

"Us?" I try to sound nonchalant, but my voice trembles slightly. "We're... figuring things out." I sigh. "Look," I start again, softer this time. "I'm not saying I have all the answers. But I do know one thing—I want to be here with you, bumps and bruises and all. And maybe that makes me a glutton for punishment, or maybe it just makes me a girl who's crazy about a certain stubborn hockey player."

"Even if he's more trouble than he's worth?"

"Especially then." I smile, my resolve strengthening. "Because for the record, Wes Jacobs, you are worth it. More than you know."

A slow grin spreads across his face, the one that's equal parts mischief and charm—the one that's been driving me mad since the day we met. "So, you're saying you love me? I'm not imagining it because of the pain meds?"

My heart skips a beat, but I don't hesitate. "Yes, you idiot, I'm saying I love you."

And just like that, the walls come down. Wes reaches for me, his touch gentle, and I lean into it, letting myself believe in this moment, in us.

"I love you too, Lexi Turner. And I swear, I'll spend every day proving it to you."

"Good," I say, settling beside him. "Because you've got a lot of penalties to make up for."

"Lexi," Wes murmurs against my lips, the previous tension melting away into something warm and right.

"Yeah?" I whisper back, my own smile impossible to contain.

"Stay with me tonight? We can watch stupid TV...and maybe not talk about hockey for once?"

"Sounds like a perfect plan," I agree, because staying here with Wes feels like the only place in the world I'm supposed to be. We're in love, actually, properly in love, and despite the comedy of errors that seems to follow us, that fact alone is enough to make everything else seem unimportant.

"Fantastic." He chuckles, and then winces again. "But maybe start with a little less contact. I'm still pretty banged up."

"Got it," I reply, laughing softly. "Minimal contact—except for this."

I lean in, pressing my lips to his in another kiss that's sweet and promising—a celebration of new beginnings and the funny way life has of bringing people together, even when they start as rivals on a cold patch of ice.

CHAPTER TWENTY FOUR: LEXI

I press my palms against the cold barrier of the Ashville Aces Arena, watching Noah and Wes glide across the ice with a focus that's both intense and careful. Eight weeks. It's been eight long weeks since their injuries sidelined them, and still, they move with an awareness of their bodies that speaks of professional athletes in tune with every ache and twinge.

The scent of fresh ice mingles with the subtle musk of exertion as I lean closer to the rink. Wes executes a gentle pivot, his shoulder obviously still tender but improving, while Noah tests the limits of his ankle with caution, his strides steady but measured. They're a picture of determination—the kind that gets under your skin and lights a fire in your chest.

"Looking good out there, boys!" I call out, unable to mask the pride swelling in my voice. They've come so far, and being a part of their journey from injury to recovery has cemented more than just my career aspirations—it's tied me to this team, to their triumphs and setbacks.

And speaking of milestones, today marks more than just another rehab session. I can't help the grin that spreads across my face as I think about the news burning a hole in my pocket. The college has officially hired me as the physical therapist for the Ashville Aces. Me, Lexi Turner, small-town girl turned key player in a professional college hockey team's behind-the-scenes hustle. Dad will be over the moon.

"Take it easy on that turn, Wes," I advise, slipping back into professional mode. "Remember what we talked about—smooth movements, no jerking."

"Got it, Coach Turner," Wes shoots back with a wink, and I roll my eyes, though my stomach does a little flip at the nickname. There's something about Wes Jacobs—the way he can be all charm one second and all concentration the next—that keeps everyone on their toes, myself included.

"Careful, Jacobs, wouldn't want you to charm yourself into another penalty box," I retort, leaning my hip against the boards, my arms crossed.

Noah laughs, circling back to join Wes. "Ignore her, she's just jealous because she can't match my coaching style."

"Your coaching style?" I scoff, arching a brow. "Let's not get ahead of ourselves, Captain. You've got to make it through my therapy sessions before you start doling out advice."

"Ouch, Lex, that's cold," Noah says, feigning hurt, but the spark in his eyes tells me he enjoys our banter as much as I do.

"Only the truth," I reply, smirking. "Now, enough chit-chat. Let's see some cross-overs, nice and slow."

They nod and push off, doing as I've instructed, their blades carving whispers into the ice. My heart swells with a mix of affection and ambition as I watch them work. This is it—the beginning of a new chapter for all of us. And I'll be damned if it isn't going to be a winning one.

I tap my clipboard against the barrier, gaze fixed on the figure skating across the ice with a measured ease that belies the strain I know he feels. "All right, Wes, let's see some lateral lunges. Remember, keep your shoulder aligned—no slacking."

Wes shoots me a grin that's all boyish charm and no repentance. "Yes, ma'am," he drawls, executing the move with a fluidity that speaks of his innate athleticism. His shoulder moves with a careful precision that speaks volumes about his recovery progress.

"Looking good, Jacobs!" I call out, unable to keep a professional note of pride from seeping into my voice. He winks in response, and I roll my eyes even as warmth colors my cheeks.

"Okay, Noah, your turn," I switch my attention to the team captain, who's been patiently waiting his turn. "Three sets of toe drags, but take it slow. We're building strength, not speed."

"Got it, boss," Noah replies, flashing me a thumbs-up before he drops his gaze to concentrate on the puck at his stick. There's something about watching him on the ice, a leader in his element, that makes my heart do a funny little skip, even though I'd never admit it out loud.

"Good form, Noah! Keep it up!" I encourage, scribbling notes onto my clipboard. They're doing well, better than expected, and a surge of satisfaction floods through me. This is why I'm here—to guide them back to their best selves, one stretch and drill at a time.

"Hey, Lexi!" Cassidy's voice cuts through the chill of the arena, and I glance over to see her striding towards me, balancing two cups of coffee in her hands. Her smile is genuine—a far cry from the forced pleasantries we used to exchange.

"Hey, Cass. What brings you here with the good stuff?" I ask, taking the offered cup and breathing in the rich aroma of freshly brewed caffeine. It's a peace offering that's become our ritual. My roommate Jenna told me to sniff the cup, and if I smell almonds, don't drink it. But Jenna watches a lot of true crime, and I doubt Cassidy is slipping me poison—she's much too sweet once you get behind the rich-girl front.

"Figured you could use a pick-me-up after playing drill sergeant with these guys," she says with a chuckle, leaning on the boards next to me. She watches Noah's practice for a moment before returning to mine. "You're really amazing with them, you know?"

I shrug, trying to play it cool despite the compliment warming me more than the coffee. "Just doing my job," I say, but I can't help the pleased tilt of my lips.

"More like working miracles," Cassidy corrects, her tone admiring. "They've come so far because of you."

"Team effort," I demur, but inside, I'm practically preening.

The cool bite of the arena air nips at my cheeks as I watch Noah glide across the ice, his movements fluid despite the lingering stiffness in his ankle. Wes is not far behind him, sending a spray of ice chips into the air with a sharp stop that makes me wince sympathetically for his shoulder. They're poetry in motion, a testament to the gritty determination that defines hockey players, and it fills me with a sense of pride.

"Can you believe Thompson's hanging up his skates early?" Cassidy muses beside me, her gaze tracking Noah's every move. There's a softness there when she looks at him, something tender and real that makes me think their relationship runs deeper than anyone expected.

I nod, sipping on my coffee. "Yeah, but it's amazing how the team's rallied. And Noah stepping in to coach next season? It speaks volumes about him."

"Definitely," she agrees, smiling proudly. "He's got this natural ability to inspire people. Plus, the extra money's a lifesaver for his family's business. He gets to heal without stressing about finances or school."

"Win-win," I say, though I can't help but worry about the pressure he's shouldering—literally and figuratively.

"Speaking of healing," Cassidy turns to me, her face clouding over with concern. "How's Wes's mom doing with her treatments?"

"Better," I reply, grateful for the question. "She's tough, like her son. They're both fighters." I leave out the part about how utterly domestic Wes and I have gotten in the past weeks; it's a blossoming romance that feels too fragile and perfect to expose to the world just yet.

"And his scholarship?" she presses gently, a frown creasing her brow.

“Still intact," I assure her, and her relief is palpable. "They're giving him time to rehab, which is more than fair. The last thing he needs is to stress about money on top of everything else."

"True," Cassidy nods, biting her lip as we turn our attention back to the ice. Noah and Wes are now racing each other, the competitive fire in their eyes sparking even in practice. It's heartening to see them so full of life, pushing each other in ways only true rivals can.

"Hey! No hot-dogging!" I call out, trying to sound stern. But my smile betrays me, and they know it. They slow down, exchanging a look that says they're not quite done showing off.

"Think they'll ever grow up?" Cassidy chuckles, and I shake my head.

"Hope not," I admit because really, their boyish charm is part of what makes them who they are. And as they skate toward us, all easy grins and playful swagger, I realize that maybe, just maybe, everything really is going to work out for the best.

I'm leaning against the cool glass of the rink, my breath fogging up a tiny circle as I watch Wes glide over the ice, his movements fluid despite the recent injury. He's always had this effortless way about him, like he's part of the rink itself—smooth, unstoppable, and so damn graceful it's almost annoying.

"Things are actually amazing," I say, turning to Cassidy, who stands beside me with two steaming cups of coffee in her hands. "Wes's mom's responding well to the chemo. The doctors think that having him nearby is really helping her fight." My lips curve into a smile when I think about the hours I've spent with her, finding out where Wes gets his stubborn streak. "You wouldn't believe how much she's like him. It's uncanny."

"Like what?" Cassidy asks, her curiosity piqued as she hands me my cup, the warmth seeping into my chilled fingers.

"Stubborn. Hopelessly optimistic. They both have this laugh that’s completely infectious." I chuckle at the thought. "And they're terrible at checkers. Absolutely no strategy whatsoever."

"Sounds like they're quite the pair," she says with a soft laugh. She sips her coffee, eyes never leaving the ice.

"Definitely," I nod.

"That's good to hear," she says genuinely, but there's something else on her mind. I can tell by the way her gaze drifts from the ice to the empty space above it, lost in thought.

"Spill it, Cass. You look like you're wrestling with some real heavy stuff," I urge, nudging her lightly with my elbow.

She takes a deep breath and then, with a mix of excitement and trepidation, spills her guts. "Noah asked me to get an apartment with him." Her cheeks bloom with a rosy flush of excitement. "My parents will have a fit when I tell them I said yes, but..." She shrugs, a brave yet vulnerable gesture. "It's my choice. My life. And honestly, Lexi? I think... I think I love him."

"Whoa," I say, the word drawn out as I process her confession. "That's huge, Cassidy. But hey, if it feels right for you, go for it."

"Really?" She searches my face for any sign of disapproval.

"Absolutely," I affirm, a genuine smile tugging at my lips. "Making decisions for yourself is important. And if Noah makes you happy, then I'm all for it."

"Thanks, Lexi." A grateful smile spreads across her face, and I can't help but feel a twinge of kinship. We've come a long way from rivals to... whatever we are now. Friends? Yeah, I'd call her a friend.

"Besides," I add with a playful wink, "you'll need someone to complain to when he leaves his dirty socks all over the place. That's what friends are for, right?"

"Right," she laughs, shaking her head. "I'll hold you to that."

"Deal," I say, clinking my coffee cup against hers.

"Deal."

"That's a big step," I add, my own thoughts drifting to Wes. Will we be making that same step next? Even with his mom, I could see it working out. I love being around her.

"An exciting one," she says, but the word gets drowned out as I stand up and lean over the boards, raising my voice to be heard over the chill of the rink.

"Hey, Noah! Extend that stride, come on!" I shout, my breath forming clouds in the cold air. My eyes are on his ankle, watching for any sign of strain. "Wes, keep that shoulder level!"

Noah pushes off with more force, his form improving as Wes glides alongside him, both of them moving in sync despite their injuries. The Ashville Aces Arena is mostly empty, the echo of puck against stick a familiar refrain. It's like music to my ears, a rhythm I've grown up with and now get to influence from my new vantage point.

"Looking good, guys!" I praise them, making a mental note of their progress.

I watch Wes and Noah exchange a look and then, almost in sync, they skate over, grinning like kids who just got away with stealing cookies.

"Looks like our presence has been requested," Cassidy observes, nudging me with an elbow. I nod, bracing myself for the incoming onslaught of charm and teasing.

"Hope they know they're not done yet," I murmur, but there's no real bite behind my words. With friends like Cassidy at my side and these guys on the mend, everything's looking up. And I wouldn't have it any other way. Noah's strides are careful but confident, a testament to his dedication to rehab, while Wes's glide is smooth, his bad-boy charm evident even from a distance.

"Time for a break?" I ask, knowing full well they're using this moment to flex their 'returning hero' muscles.

"Something like that," Wes shoots back, a grin spreading across his face, those ice-blue eyes locking onto mine with a hint of mischief.

Noah reaches us first, Cassidy's face lighting up in a way that rivals the arena's floodlights. "I believe this belongs to you," he says, blowing her a kiss with an exaggerated bow that has me biting back a laugh.

"Careful there, Mr. Coach," Cassidy teases, pretending to catch the kiss. "Don't want you injuring that ankle before you even start your new career."

"Ah, but if I did, I'd have the best physical therapist and her trusty assistant on my case," Noah replies, his gaze sliding over to me with a grin.

"Trusty assistant?" Wes scoffs, coming to a stop beside Noah. He wraps an arm around my waist, pulling me close enough to feel the chill from his jersey through my jacket. "Lexi's the brains behind this operation. You're just the brawn."

"Hey!" Noah mock protests, but Cassidy silences him with a kiss that's both congratulatory and possessive, her fingers curling into the fabric of his practice jersey.

"Get a room, you two," I joke, rolling my eyes for effect though warmth fills me at their easy affection.

"Jealous?" Wes murmurs into my ear, skating up to blow his breath warm against my skin.

"Of them?" I quip, tilting my head to look at him. "Please, we've got way more chemistry than a high school lab class."

"Is that so?" Wes challenges with a raised eyebrow.

"Undeniable." I stand on my tiptoes, closing the gap between us. His lips meet mine in a kiss that's equal parts tender and teasing—a perfect blend of our personalities. It's a kiss full of promises, of late-night study sessions turned make-out marathons, of silent support in crowded rooms, and loud cheers from the bleachers.

We break apart, breathless but grinning like fools. "That's what I thought," Wes says, his voice low and satisfied.

"Okay, lovebirds, break it up," Cassidy calls out, her laughter echoing off the empty stands. "Save some romance for the rest of us."

"Sorry, Cass," I say, not sorry at all as I lace my fingers with Wes's. "But when you've got it, you flaunt it."

"Speaking of flaunting," Noah adds, looking between us with a smirk, "how about we take this victory lap together?"

"Sounds like a plan," Wes agrees, and we all step onto the ice. The four of us skate side by side, our laughter mingling with the sound of blades cutting across the rink.

It's a moment suspended in time, where everything is right in our little world. The struggles we've faced—my own injuries, Noah's family business, Wes's mom's health, and Cassidy breaking free from her parents' expectations—all seem distant now. Here, gliding over the smooth surface, there's no past or future, only the present and the people we share it with.

As the lights of the Ashville Aces Arena shine down on us, I can't help but think that this is what happiness feels like—unexpected, overwhelming, and entirely ours.

NOW AVAILABLE!

ICY INTIMACY
(An Ashville Aces Hockey Romance—Book 2)

"This is a clean contemporary romance that you will find hard to put down!"
--Amazon reviewer (regarding Always, Forever)

ICY INTIMACY is the second book in a spellbinding new sports romance series by Fiona Grace, #1 bestselling author of Murder in the Manor, which has over 10,000 five star reviews!

In picturesque Ashville, Minnesota, the ice may be cold but hockey gets heated at Ashville College.

When **fiery journalism major Samantha Kelly** crosses her editor, she's **relegated to the sports beat**—specifically, the Ashville Aces hockey team.

While chronicling their games, **Sam finds herself drawn to a respectable defenseman** whose integrity and wits catch her off guard. But **the team's infamous winger**, a reckless playboy who thrives in the limelight, **is determined to score her attention**.

Caught between sincerity and seduction, will she expose her heart's winning shot? Or will love be benched in this game of contrasts?

Prepare to be captivated by the ASHVILLE ACES, where a fusion of sporty action and romantic adventures beckons, leading you to a charming setting replete with witty banter, heartfelt moments, and unexpected twists. Alluring new protagonists in each book will steal your heart and have you reading late into the night.

Future books in the series are now available!

"Very entertaining. I highly recommend this book to the permanent library of any reader that appreciates a very well written mystery, with some twists and an intelligent plot. You will not be disappointed. Excellent way to spend a cold weekend!"
--Books and Movie Reviews, Roberto Mattos (regarding *Murder in the Manor*)

"The story line wasn't just a who done it, but had a story about her life and romance, including village life. Very entertaining."
--Amazon reviewer (regarding *Murder in the Manor*)

"It has endearing and sometimes quirky characters, a plot that keeps you reading and the right amount of romance. I can't wait to start book two!"
--Amazon reviewer (regarding *Murder in the Manor*)

"What a great story of murder, romance, new beginnings, love, friend ships and a wonderful cascade of mystery."
--Amazon reviewer (regarding *Murder in the Manor*)

"A bit of romance and a very determined woman! I have read many of Fiona Grace's novels and loved every one of them—this was no exception. I am looking forward to reading the rest of this new series!"
--Amazon reviewer (regarding *Always, With You*)

Fiona Grace

Fiona Grace is author of the LACEY DOYLE COZY MYSTERY series, comprising nine books; of the TUSCAN VINEYARD COZY MYSTERY series, comprising seven books; of the DUBIOUS WITCH COZY MYSTERY series, comprising three books; of the BEACHFRONT BAKERY COZY MYSTERY series, comprising six books; of the CATS AND DOGS COZY MYSTERY series, comprising nine books; of the ELIZA MONTAGU COZY MYSTERY series, comprising nine books (and counting); of the ENDLESS HARBOR ROMANTIC COMEDY series, comprising nine books (and counting); of the INN AT DUNE ISLAND ROMANTIC COMEDY series, comprising seven books (and counting); of the INN BY THE SEA ROMANTIC COMEDY series, comprising five books (and counting); of the MAID AND THE MANSION COZY MYSTERY series, comprising five books (and counting); of the ALICE BLOOM COZY MYSTERY series, comprising five books (and counting); of the MAGNOLIA BAY COZY MYSTERY series, comprising five books (and counting); of the TIMBERLAKE TITANS HOCKEY ROMANCE series, comprising five books (and counting); and of the ASHVILLE ACES HOCKEY ROMANCE series, comprising five books (and counting).

Fiona would love to hear from you, so please visit www.fionagraceauthor.com to receive free ebooks, hear the latest news, and stay in touch.

BOOKS BY FIONA GRACE

ASHVILLE ACES HOCKEY ROMANCE
BREAKAWAY BLISS (Book #1)
ICY INTIMACY (Book #2)
FACEOFF FLING (Book #3)
RINK RENDEZVOUS (Book #4)
HOCKEY HEARTTHROB (Book #5)

TIMBERLAKE TITANS HOCKEY ROMANCE
RINKSIDE ROMANCE (Book #1)
FLIRTY FACEOFF (Book #2)
MELTING THE ICE (Book #3)
THE PUCK STOPS HERE (Book #4)
GLOVES DROP, LOVE BLOOMS (Book #5)

MAGNOLIA BAY COZY MYSTERY
THE TAINTED TAFFY (Book #1)
A MASKED MURDER (Book #2)
A CAFE CONFESSION (Book #3)
THE FROZEN FIND (Book #4)
A CURIOUS CURSE (Book #5)

THE MAID AND THE MANSION COZY MYSTERY
A MYSTERIOUS MURDER (Book #1)
A SCANDALOUS DEATH (Book #2)
A MISSING GUEST (Book #3)
AN UNSOLVABLE CRIME (Book #4)
AN IMPOSSIBLE HEIST (Book #5)

INN BY THE SEA ROMANTIC COMEDY
A NEW LOVE (Book #1)
A NEW CHANCE (Book #2)
A NEW HOME (Book #3)
A NEW LIFE (Book #4)
A NEW ME (Book #5)

THE INN AT DUNE ISLAND ROMANTIC COMEDY
A CHANCE LOVE (Book #1)
A CHANCE FALL (Book #2)
A CHANCE ROMANCE (Book #3)
A CHANCE CHRISTMAS (Book #4)
A CHANCE ENGAGEMENT (Book #5)
A CHANCE DREAM (Book #6)
A CHANCE WEDDING (Book #7)

ENDLESS HARBOR ROMANTIC COMEDY
ALWAYS, WITH YOU (Book #1)
ALWAYS, FOREVER (Book #2)
ALWAYS, PLUS ONE (Book #3)
ALWAYS, TOGETHER (Book #4)
ALWAYS, LIKE THIS (Book #5)
ALWAYS, FATED (Book #6)
ALWAYS, FOR LOVE (Book #7)
ALWAYS, JUST US (Book #8)
ALWAYS, IN LOVE (Book #9)

ELIZA MONTAGU COZY MYSTERY
MURDER AT THE HEDGEROW (Book #1)
A DALLOP OF DEATH (Book #2)
CALAMITY AT THE BALL (Book #3)
A SPEAKEASY DEMISE (Book #4)
A FLAPPER FATALITY (Book #5)
BUMPED BY A DAME (Book #6)
A DOLL'S DEBACLE (Book #7)
A FELLA'S RUIN (Book #8)
A GAL'S OFFING (Book #9)

LACEY DOYLE COZY MYSTERY
MURDER IN THE MANOR (Book#1)
DEATH AND A DOG (Book #2)
CRIME IN THE CAFE (Book #3)
VEXED ON A VISIT (Book #4)
KILLED WITH A KISS (Book #5)
PERISHED BY A PAINTING (Book #6)
SILENCED BY A SPELL (Book #7)
FRAMED BY A FORGERY (Book #8)
CATASTROPHE IN A CLOISTER (Book #9)

TUSCAN VINEYARD COZY MYSTERY
AGED FOR MURDER (Book #1)
AGED FOR DEATH (Book #2)
AGED FOR MAYHEM (Book #3)
AGED FOR SEDUCTION (Book #4)
AGED FOR VENGEANCE (Book #5)
AGED FOR ACRIMONY (Book #6)
AGED FOR MALICE (Book #7)

DUBIOUS WITCH COZY MYSTERY
SKEPTIC IN SALEM: AN EPISODE OF MURDER (Book #1)
SKEPTIC IN SALEM: AN EPISODE OF CRIME (Book #2)
SKEPTIC IN SALEM: AN EPISODE OF DEATH (Book #3)

BEACHFRONT BAKERY COZY MYSTERY
BEACHFRONT BAKERY: A KILLER CUPCAKE (Book #1)
BEACHFRONT BAKERY: A MURDEROUS MACARON (Book #2)
BEACHFRONT BAKERY: A PERILOUS CAKE POP (Book #3)
BEACHFRONT BAKERY: A DEADLY DANISH (Book #4)
BEACHFRONT BAKERY: A TREACHEROUS TART (Book #5)
BEACHFRONT BAKERY: A CALAMITOUS COOKIE (Book #6)

CATS AND DOGS COZY MYSTERY
A VILLA IN SICILY: OLIVE OIL AND MURDER (Book #1)
A VILLA IN SICILY: FIGS AND A CADAVER (Book #2)
A VILLA IN SICILY: VINO AND DEATH (Book #3)
A VILLA IN SICILY: CAPERS AND CALAMITY (Book #4)
A VILLA IN SICILY: ORANGE GROVES AND VENGEANCE (Book #5)
A VILLA IN SICILY: CANNOLI AND A CASUALTY (Book #6)

ALICE BLOOM COZY MYSTERY
MURDER IN THE MARIGOLDS (Book #1)
RUIN IN THE ROSES (Book #2)
DECEIT IN THE DAFFODILS (Book #3)
SCANDAL IN THE SAFFRON (Book #4)
CATASTROPHE IN THE CARNATIONS (Book #5)

Printed in Great Britain
by Amazon

48118049R00083